ONE PER COFFIN

Tony Block

One Per Coffin is a work of fiction. Names, characters, places, and incidents either are the product of the author's imagination or are used fictitiously. Any resemblance to actual persons, living or dead, events, or locales is entirely coincidental.

ISBN-13: 978-0-692-86480-7

This one is for Dean

ONE

The prison guard pushed me into the chair, cuffed my hands and feet to the table, checked his work twice and, closing the door behind him, left the room.

The room was brick and white paint, a metal table and two metal chairs. The table and chairs were bolted to the floor, so if an inmate got upset, he wouldn't have anything within reach to beat his lawyer. I met my lawyer in here twice. After the second time he stopped coming, so I stopped coming. I never wanted to hit him with a chair, a table maybe.

The door opened and a man wearing a rumpled suit sat down across from me. He wore the suit like an afterthought —something put on to let the dog outside at night. Puffy sacks drooped his eyes and he smelled like cigarettes. He opened a manila folder with a fighter's hand—meaty fingers and scarred knuckles. Though his face needed shaving and his teeth needed brushing, the eyes were intelligent. His hair was damp, which meant either snow or rain. I wasn't certain of the season or the month. Twelve years in a cell does that.

I held up the handcuffs.

"That's funny," he said.

I shrugged.

"My name is Detective Munroe. You can call me *Detective* Munroe. I'd like to start this interview by talking about Boris Egorov."

When I said nothing, he asked, "Would you like to talk about Georgy Chorkina instead?"

I glanced at the stack of paper. The top sheet was old and yellow and the text looked stamped from a typewriter, not a form spit from a computer.

He said, "I will tell you what I know and then you tell me what you know. It's simpler that way. It builds trust." He rubbed his jaw and glanced at the sheet of paper. "Twelve years ago, you shot Boris Egorov twice in the chest with a .38 caliber revolver killing him. You ran, but we caught you like cops do. Now you're in prison. Simple story. Not complicated. You've been here a long time."

"What is this about?"

"We have new evidence showing you didn't shoot Egorov. We now believe it was Georgy Chorkina who pulled the trigger."

"I killed Egorov. If Georgy said he did it, he's lying."

"What happened to the revolver?"

"I don't know. I ran. The police found me standing by the river with empty hands. I might have taken the gun, I might not. I was in shock."

Munroe flipped the top sheet and read from the next. "We dredged the river but didn't find the gun. That time of year the water was low so it should have been easy to find. Did you go there often?"

"The river? Yeah, if the weather was good I'd go on my lunch breaks and watch the boats."

"You cooperated with the police. You helped them in every way you could."

I shrugged. "I killed him. He was an asshole, but he didn't deserve to die. Not like that, not over a drunken misunderstanding."

"Why were you there that night?"

"Egorov needed parts to repair the cars. He bought them wholesale from manufacturers and part stores. I drove his delivery truck to get them or return them as needed. That day we were busy, and I didn't finish my runs until late."

"How long did you work for Egorov?"

"Three months."

"And at no time did you see him involved in any kind of drug dealing?"

I sighed. The same question everyone asks eventually. He got to it quicker than most. "No, I didn't know he dealt drugs. I delivered parts and that was it."

"You never looked in the packages you delivered?"

"Every time I saw a delivery package I saw parts. I never once thought of drugs. Some Egorov put in paper, some in boxes. They weighed what I expected them to weigh, so I didn't become suspicious. I'd go to the part store, drop off the package or pick it up, get a receipt and head back to the shop."

Munroe flipped to the next page. "How do you know Georgy Chorkina?"

"He was one of Egorov's mechanics. He was an asshole. They were all assholes. They drank and argued and sometimes beat each other up. It was a weird Russian thing I didn't understand. I took the job because I wanted to work on cars. I tried to get them to teach me, but they ignored me because I was American."

"We found the gun used to kill Egorov."

"And?"

"We didn't find it in the river. We found it in a storage unit Chorkina had rented for the last twelve years."

"He's in prison."

"Ten years. Serving a life sentence for beating a man to death in a bar fight."

"So what?"

"The gun has his prints all over it, not yours."

"After twelve years I wouldn't expect to find them. Maybe I dropped the gun at the scene. Maybe somebody grabbed it before the cops came and somewhere along the way Chorkina got ahold of it. Maybe he uses it to scare his kids on Halloween: *The Gun That Killed Boris Egorov.*"

Munroe grunted. "Chorkina doesn't have kids."

I shrugged. "That was the only theory I had."

"Chorkina admitted to killing Egorov. He gave us the gun and the ballistics matched."

"He didn't kill Egorov. I did."

"He claims he found Egorov beating on you and tried to stop him. Egorov went at him with a crowbar so he pulled the gun and shot him twice in the chest."

"Egorov abused everyone. One guy he beat so bad he broke his own hand and they both ended up in the hospital. Chorkina didn't care about me or anybody else. He would have stood by and watched if Egorov used me as a punching bag. He sure as hell wouldn't have pulled a gun on Egorov."

"Makes more sense than the mess at your trial."

"The DA didn't like me."

"She had a career case in Egorov. Convicting him would let her walk straight up to the Attorney General's office. Only that didn't happen. You put two holes in her Russian drug dealer. Two bullets killed a man and a career." He scratched at his ear. "She got petty, took it out on you. Nobody believed you were gunning for Egorov's job, but she wanted you prosecuted and you got prosecuted. Now you're here enjoying the finest of penitentiary accommodations."

"I get the upper bunk and apple pie." I sat forward in the chair. Munroe smelled like a wet ashtray. "What does Chorkina get for claiming to kill Egorov? The Russians know I killed him. They send someone after me every couple of years as a reminder. Does Chorkina have family or somebody he's supporting?"

In his late fifties, Chorkina had spent most of his adult life involved in one criminal activity or another. The only down time he had was during incarceration. He didn't need money, not like somebody who has their freedom needs money. Maybe he had a family member who needed help. Tacking on another twenty years wouldn't matter if somebody important got a sizable chunk of money. Maybe it was supposed to make up for past transgressions on his part.

"This isn't about Chorkina," Munroe said. "It's about you. Chorkina gave himself up, so you go free. He gave us everything we need to prosecute him, which nullifies your conviction."

"Not all the evidence points at Chorkina though. They used audio tapes at my trial. The recordings confirm the argument between me and Egorov. Cocaine found at the scene matched cocaine on my shirt where Egorov hit me. And they had my confession."

"A confession we're treating as suspect. Look at this from a different angle. Maybe Chorkina paid you to take the fall. The plan was for you to plead self-defense. Much easier for you than for him. No criminal record, new to the city, pregnant girlfriend. Why would a jury convict you? But it didn't work that way and you went to prison. Maybe in his old age he's feeling guilty, wants to atone for his sins."

5

"Egorov could have ground my skull into the ground and Chorkina would have stood by watching. He wouldn't feel guilt killing a bus full of nuns. And he sure as hell wouldn't take credit for killing Egorov not if he didn't do it. Not with Egorov's brother out there."

Munroe flipped through his paperwork and came up with a photo. Grainy and smudged, it showed the backs of three men walking through a warehouse.

"The one in the middle is Boris's brother, Petr. He was released from prison last week. The Russians claim it's due to overcrowding, but the truth is we stopped paying them to keep him incarcerated. The new administration policy is to give criminals a spare room in the White House, not keep them in prison."

I sat back in the chair and exhaled. The metal links of the handcuffs clinked together and sounded loud in the small room. "I killed Egorov."

Munroe laughed. "Hell, Brogan, I *know* you did. There's no doubt in my mind. Egorov was drunk that night. He cut the coke wrong and blamed you for the bad weight. I believe you when you say you didn't know about the drugs. I think you were naïve and so focused on your own problems you didn't see what was going on around you. The entire situation was a farce. Egorov got himself killed because he couldn't weigh a bag of cocaine and you got a life sentence because you couldn't see he was a drug dealer."

He jammed his finger onto the photo of Petr Egorov. "But this guy, he's a different problem. He's so interested in meeting you he's willing to risk coming here so he can put a bullet in your head." He turned the photo around so I could see it. "You're going to help me catch him, because he's your get of jail card."

I looked at the photo of three men wearing heavy dark

overcoats. The two on the left had broad shoulders and the one on the right had rounded shoulders. The photo made their hair dark, but the one with rounded shoulders looked like it might be graying. I couldn't see their faces, nor could I tell their height. The photo clipped them at the waist. They faced heavy machinery, a backhoe maybe. The one on the left pointed a gloved hand off to the left of the frame. "What happens to my conviction?"

"It'll be overturned. If you cooperate *this* District Attorney won't retry the case. Once the paperwork is processed, the felony gets removed from your record. You'll be nineteen all over again."

"Only I'm thirty-one."

"Well, you *killed* the guy. That should count for something. You *could* count yourself lucky that the brother of the man you killed is so motivated to meet you. Without his help, you'd still be in prison."

"What about a gun?"

"You get within ten feet of a revolver, a semi-automatic, a rifle—hell, if I see a water gun—I'll drag your ass back in here. I don't care if you're on your knees with Petr sticking a barrel down your throat, you don't pick up a gun, you hear me? That route puts you right back in here."

"Can I use my fists?"

He closed the folder and stood. "Petr Egorov is coming and I want him. You don't do *anything* but sit around looking pretty."

"I'm bait."

"Yes, you are. See, how this works is the minute you're dead, he goes back to work taking over the drug trade, which means bodies in the street. Me, I'd like to legalize every drug on the street, but that's above my pay grade. What is within my pay grade is following him around until he kills somebody. Then I can put handcuffs on him. Not too tight because we don't want to violate his civil rights, but tight enough he can't get away. You're going to make that happen. I'm going to dangle you out on a line, parade you around town in a pink jumpsuit if I must, and when he takes his shot at you I'm going to be there to put a bullet in his head. You should thank me, Brogan, not give me attitude."

"You going to take these handcuffs off now?"

TWO

We watched snow fall from inside Munroe's car while the heater belched cool air through the defroster. The heater did little to warm the car and even less to clear the windshield. Every fifteen minutes Munroe would complain, climb from the car and slap the blades to clear the slush streaking across glass.

Back at the prison Munroe had stuffed me in a suit too tight in the shoulders and too long in the sleeves, gave me a thrift store coat that smelled of a highway underpass and declared me ready to return to civilization. Now he stared through the grimy windshield, lit another cigarette—his fifth since we'd parked at the bus terminal—and lowered his window. He exhaled and watched the smoke dissipate through the crack while I sat on fast food wrappers and itched in dirty wool.

A digital sign announced my bus would arrive in five minutes.

Munroe swore. "That's the sixth delay already. What the hell is happening to this city?"

He flicked his cigarette into the snow and pulled a packet from his pocket, which he stared at before handing to me. The packet contained a bus pass, a list of names and telephone numbers and a small stack of bills.

"That's a lot of money," I said.

He snorted. "You *have* been gone a long time. That won't get you anywhere we can't find you. Remember, you don't have a passport or any kind of identification. You're not going anywhere we don't want you going."

"Why not leave me in prison?"

He lit another cigarette. "Get yourself a motel room, a cold beer, watch some television and go to work. Stay out of sight for two weeks. We'll capture Egorov and you'll be a free man. Just keep your head on and don't run."

Keep your head on.

"Are you expecting him to come after me with a machete?"

He stared at me, his eyes bloodshot from the cigarette smoke.

I put the money and paper in my pocket and noticed the sign announcing the bus would be late again. Munroe glanced at his watch. The analog hands displayed four o'clock. He wore no wedding ring, and this car wasn't fit for date night, so I wondered where he needed to be.

"Why the hurry?" I asked.

"Why what hurry? You think I like hanging out at bus stops in the middle of the night with convicts? I want sleep."

"Good plan. You look like you haven't slept in a week. That's not all of it though. You're chain smoking to stay awake and you're babysitting me onto a bus instead of driving me. Something else is going on."

"We have one week once Egorov arrives. We need to be ready."

We?

The terminal sign lit up announcing my bus.

"How many people do you have on your team?"

He didn't answer.

"*How many people?*"

"We won't have anyone on you directly but we'll be watching."

"*How?* I'm not wearing a wire and you won't be close. How are you going to help me if someone comes along to kill me? Do I just yell real loud?"

"Shut up, Brogan."

"This is your plan? You'll *watch* me? Please tell me you didn't graduate at the top of your class. How close is your nearest team?"

"Thirty minutes."

"You'll be *thirty minutes* away? So, what you're telling me is, I'm on my own, right? Is that what you're telling me?"

"You done?"

"I'd like to go on record stating my lack of support for this *plan.*"

"I don't give a damn about your support."

He chain lit another cigarette and pushed the old butt out the window. It hissed out before hitting the ground.

I thought about time. I thought about twelve years in prison kind of time. I thought about all those minutes spent staring at a clock wishing the seconds could move faster to get me to a minute like now, where I was free, and now feeling like I didn't have the time to figure out all the details I needed to know to make decisions.

"You don't want this going Federal," I said, "because the minute he steps on US soil the DEA steps in and you're shut down. You need to get Egorov fast and you need to keep it local. But why? So you get the credit? What else? What is

Egorov to you, Munroe? Why you so interested in him?"

"Get on the bus, go to the address on the paper, do the job interview. Lou Kelly owns the repair shop. You can work on his cars for the next couple of weeks. Just keep your mouth shut, *please.*"

"There anything along the route? It won't take me four hours to get to the shop."

"There's an all-night diner a couple blocks from the shop. Go there and get a bite. Lou should be in around eight."

"I know him. I met him once long ago."

Munroe was silent. After a minute, he nodded. "I didn't make that connection but I can see it. He was a competitor back in the day. Well, I worked a deal with him—told him you were just released from prison. He didn't act surprised which connects with him knowing you. Don't talk to him about details. Just go to work like everybody else. We'll watch for Egorov."

"What if his people get me instead?"

"Won't happen. Egorov wants you himself. If he's not in country, they'll leave you alone. They see you take a local job, they won't think you're spooked."

"I'm feeling better already."

"Remember, I'm the cavalry. You want me to come, you play nice."

I took a deep breath, sat up straight in the seat and faced Munroe. "There's not a chance in hell I'll call you. What happens next you'll watch from the sidelines. Petr Egorov is gunning for me, he wants me dead. You want me to shut up and sit in my corner but I won't do that. I'm going to be loud and I'm going to be mean and I'm going to shine a light on every dark corner until I find this guy and put a bullet in his head."

I opened the door and stepped out of the car. "You're a

cop and you're thinking about your career. Maybe you're honest, maybe you're not. You'll prove it either way soon enough. And I'll say this slow so you can understand it: Don't worry about me running away because I won't. I'm going to be front and center and anybody who tries to come after me will bleed for it."

The bus pulled into the terminal stopping at the gate.

Munroe chewed on the end of his cigarette trying to figure out what to say but I didn't give him a chance. I closed the door and climbed onto the bus.

I told the driver the address and asked if he could get me there even with the snow. He nodded and that suited me. I found a bench and hunkered down to think.

A lot had happened in the last twenty-four hours. Even more would happen in the next two weeks. I needed to find a place to hole up and make plans. When they came for me, the situation would get ugly fast.

I thought about Boris Egorov. He used me because I was a dumb kid who was easily manipulated. He didn't care about hurting me or anyone else. People like that *will* hurt you. And the less you pay attention the more damage they do. But I got lucky back then, when I defended myself and ended up killing him. The court decided I was wrong and I lost twelve years of my life.

Now his brother was loose and wanted me dead. His men tried several times on the inside. I hadn't been fast enough the first time—I didn't even realize these kinds of things happened—and took a knife in the gut. I spent several months in the infirmary. Munroe was right: I *had been* dumb. But laying in that hospital bed, I made a promise to myself that I'd get smarter, that I'd get faster and that I wouldn't let them hurt me any longer. I played things smart. Egorov's men came after me a couple more times, and they had gotten me alone and had broken bones, but not the third time. The third time, I walked away and they didn't. They stopped coming after that. After a while I wondered if Egorov had given up but that was wishful thinking. He would come for me and I knew it. It was just a matter of time. Killing his brother was personal. He *had* to respond. Would I be any different if I had a brother?

I fell asleep and woke up to the driver yelling at me from the front of the bus. My eyeballs burned and my body felt heavy. Waving at him to shut the hell up took all my energy. While I stifled a yawn, he scowled at me in the rearview mirror.

It was still dark out and a foot of snow had fallen in the night. The street had seen a plow in the last hour but the side streets were impassable. How the driver got this far, I didn't know.

I stopped next to him and said, "Thanks."

He gave me a look that said any time I wanted to shove off would be just fine with him. He was about my size, smaller in the chest and shorter overall, but it was hard to tell with him sitting forward in the seat his hand on the door opener.

I gave him Kelly's address and asked, "How far from here?"

I must have been a sight worth pitying because he said, "Mister, there's nothing out there. You try to walk anywhere in them clothes and you won't make it."

A woman smiled from an advertisement on the back of the bus stop bench. Wearing a summer dress, she ran along a golden beach, her legs long and tan. The other half of the advertisement hid under a discolored layer of ice so thick I couldn't tell what made the woman smile.

Cars lined the streets like huge sleeping snowmen. A street lamp at the end of the block cast a yellowish glow onto heaps of trash peaking from beneath drifts of snow.

"That coat and those shoes won't get you far. You want, ride to the station, maybe you can find a place to sleep there."

"Thanks for the sympathy, friend, but I'll walk."

I pulled my coat tighter but made no real effort for the door.

"You know," he said by way of filling the silence, "a guy with a face like you, I figure you were in the military or maybe you were just born with it. Either way that makes you one unlucky son of a bitch."

"Unlucky is only half of it."

"What gets you out here so late in this weather?"

"A job interview," I said.

"Must be a hell of a job. You should buy a better coat with your first paycheck, that one smells."

I stood there for another minute.

He gave me a look and a shrug that said he had to do what he had to do. He opened the door. Icy wind scraped my face and cut through my coat blowing away any pockets of warmth. I stepped down onto the sidewalk. Burning cold numbed my toes. Melted snow clung to my pants, stiffening them into a hard shell. My leg muscles tightened in spasm that worked up through my back.

"Which way?" I asked.

He pointed north. "You got ten blocks of walking through a foot of snow. Three blocks that way, seven east."

I looked down the street and saw an empty wasteland of derelicts and snow.

"You staying or going?"

I pulled up my collar and waved him away. He closed the door and I started walking. For the next block, I could hear him gunning the engine trying to clear the bus from the snow. He must have finally gotten it because after the next block the only sounds I heard were a distant train and stinging wind.

Thick snowflakes floated from the gray sky above filling me with claustrophobia. I wanted to crouch under the edge of a building and light a fire, never to move again. But I couldn't stop. Stopping would mean defeat; stopping would mean the cold froze my blood and ended my life, because I had no fire and no way to make one. So I walked and I ignored the pain in my legs and my hands and my chest. Walking under a street light, where the snow turned a yellow-gray, I wondered why the copper cables pumping electricity didn't snap. I wondered why I didn't snap.

Up one street and down another, I moved diagonally across town. By the next block my feet lost sensation, and I stumbled more than once on curbs I couldn't see. I stuffed my hands as far into the pockets as I could get them, but it wasn't enough to keep the cold from seeping into them and freezing them. I couldn't let it matter though. I couldn't stand still.

So I walked.

The neighborhood was a cross between revitalized and broken down, a curious mixture of auto shops, foundries and converted offices. The offices had whole brick walls removed and replaced with thick sheets of glass showing designer furniture and large screen computers. Several buildings retained brick walls advertising the buildings' original purposes: textiles, hardware, lumber. But soon those renovations faded out. What was left were worn down houses and corner markets boarded up and marked with graffiti. Piles of snow covering trash filled the occasional empty lot. All of it was crushed under the winter cold.

The river was about six blocks north, a winding snake that

effectively divided the rich and the dead. This side had the warehouses and burned-out husks, that side had the towers and lights. Occasionally I caught glimpses of them through the snowfall, fuzzy reds, greens and blues all mashed together.

No cars passed me on the road, the snow was too deep on these streets. A truck might have made it, but the driver would need a hell of a reason.

I hunched forward imprisoned in a new cage. This one cold like I'd never experienced. I wanted to stretch my arms and feel my freedom but I felt no freedom. I was as trapped here as in a prison cell.

The walls were gone and their loss frightened me. For twelve years, wherever I turned, they were an inescapable constant. And now part of me wanted to go back to them to embrace their certainty, their security and their warmth.

That filled me with a white-hot anger with nothing to direct it at, at least not tonight, but soon. For now, I had to focus on other things, the first being a job. I'd taken up shop work in prison, eventually working on cars, mostly the state vehicles around the prison. I liked the work but hated the vehicles. It was honest work and honest was the only thing I had.

I nearly walked past the body shop. The sign hanging over two broad barn doors was unlit under a cover of snow. It was only because I noticed the address numbers made of four big blocks of wood that made me stop. The numbers, hammered onto the wall over the doors, were painted a sloppy red which had dripped down on to the doors like blood. The place looked ready to collapse in on itself.

I was shaking uncontrollably. I'd pushed myself too hard getting here but I couldn't have stayed still at the bus station or anywhere else. I had sat idle too long but now I was free and I had to go somewhere, accomplish something, only this wasn't what I'd expected to come to. Munroe had been wrong. No coffee shops, no diners, were in this part of town any longer. This part of town was dead, and I would be too if I didn't find heat.

The overhead light snapped on illuminating the sign *Kelly's Body Shop*. It went off, on, off again. It wasn't a faulty circuit. Somebody was playing with the switch.

The words faded into darkness and I had to blink to clear the spots. No tire tracks. The building sat on a corner, with several snow-covered cars lining the street. I walked down to the end of the building and around the corner.

That's when I saw the pickup truck.

THREE

The twenty-year-old truck idled loudly in the cold winter night. Snow crunched under my feet as I walked up to the open driver's side window. The cab was empty and the heater was on high. I leaned in and let the warmth wash over me like a hot shower. I swayed slightly, dizzied from the contrasting temperatures. The nerves in my legs burned and my hands shook uncontrollably. I pushed them through the window to get closer to the heat. Country music played on the radio but it couldn't distract me from the pain in my body. I opened the door to get closer to the heater.

Muffled laughter came from inside the shop. I stopped, listening. More muffled sounds. I turned the radio off. The truck's headlights lit up a rusty side door. It had given up with one hell of a fight. Foot long splinters of wood from the doorframe littered the ground like upended toothpicks.

I considered stealing the truck and driving as far south as Munroe's money would take me. But I knew I couldn't do it. Running would put me back in prison; I had told Munroe the truth: I wanted my life back.

I approached the door, stood to one side and listened through the gap. Somebody belched and cursed and somebody else laughed and grunted while a tarp scraped across concrete and tools crashed to the floor.

If somebody came out the door I was in no shape to stop him. The heater hadn't thawed me out, but maybe being numb was an advantage. If I hit first, maybe I wouldn't have to worry about picking myself up off the ground.

I guessed there were only two of them. If they had guns and I rushed through the door, they'd shoot me dead. But I didn't think guns were likely. If they had planned to steal property, they would have parked the truck away from the door, not towards it. They were here to damage the place, not take anything. That made junkies or thieves unlikely. Troublemaking teens possibly. That would explain the age and the quality of the truck. And professionals didn't laugh like that. Kids being stupid did.

The plan was simple: enter fast, hit the nearest one as hard as I could, and then take out his buddy.

I charged through the door.

I was wrong. Two men in their twenties, not high school kids, looked up at my arrival. The one on the left had blond hair and held a crowbar. It must have been fifteen degrees outside, but he wore a t-shirt and faded jeans. The one on the right had black hair and stood next to a drum of used engine oil. He wore a grease stained canvas work coat and held a box of matches in his hands.

The two were about the same distance apart from me and saw me as I came in. Blond stood on the hood of a car with the crowbar poised to smash the windshield. Black lit one of the matches and stared at it with a stupid expression on his face. I moved towards him.

Blond grinned and brought the crowbar down on the

windshield. Chips of glass flew in every direction. He glanced at me, got no reaction, grinned and did it again two more times. He stood up, howled to the ceiling and wiped sweat from his puffy face like this was the most strenuous effort he'd exerted in a long time, or ever.

Black flicked the match onto the oil drum where it promptly went out. He frowned, not knowing it takes more than a match to light engine oil. I was almost on him when he dropped the box of matches and picked up a fourteen-inch pipe wrench from the workbench behind him. He had it over his shoulder by the time I was on him. I gave him a punch in the nose backed by all my bodyweight. His head snapped back, he bounced off the workbench and fell to his knees. The pipe wrench hit the floor next to him.

Blond jumped from the hood of the car towards me from the side. I moved out of the way and he tumbled into a cart full of shop tools. The cart fell forward and the shop erupted in a cacophony.

I started forward to be there ready before he got up when Black popped up like a marionette on a string. His unfocused eyes glistened from his blood covered face like two runny eggs. He lurched towards me with his hands out. He grabbed my shirt with a weak grip and tried to pull me backwards but I didn't move. I hit him in the face again, this time with a hard roundhouse from the right side. His head snapped left and blood flew from his mouth. He made a groaning sucking sound as he fell to the floor.

Blond stood up and laughed at me. "You're a stupid son of a bitch, you know that? You know who you messed with? He's going to kill you once he finds out. You're one dead dude!"

He didn't give me time to respond. He'd found the pipe wrench and swung it faster than I expected. I used my arm to block it from taking my head off. I didn't feel the pain then but I knew I would later. I ran forward, slammed him into the workbench and brought my elbow up under his chin. His head snapped back and he fell to the floor.

Black popped back up again.

"What the hell are you on?" I asked.

He grinned. One of his teeth sat crooked in his bloody mouth. He tried to talk, but spit blood and saliva instead.

I ran at him plowing into him as hard as I could. He went down and this time his head bounced off the concrete and I knew he wouldn't be getting back up. Two fuzzy, colorless eyes stared up at me and I wondered if I had killed him.

I didn't get time to check, because Blond hit me from behind and this time he connected with my head. I fell forward landing on my hands and knees. My vision dimmed. I needed to vomit. Blond danced around me laughing hysterically before swinging his leg in a kick that hit square in my gut. I rolled to my side and tumbled into the pit. I barely got my arms up in time to protect my face before hitting the bottom and blacking out.

FOUR

"And that's how it happened?" Lou Kelly asked.

"That's not enough for you?"

It was a little after eight. I should have been walking through the door all bright and nervous like a kid at his first job interview. Instead, I sat on a bench with a snow-filled towel pressed to the back of my head.

Kelly had found me unconscious, woke me with a couple of hard shoves and asked my name. When I told him, he nodded, grabbed a beat up military med kit and proceeded to patch my skull. He did a decent job. I no longer felt nauseous and could see without spots dancing across my vision.

Now we were sitting in his office with him behind the desk and me trying not to bleed on anything. Not that I was worried; blood would give the place color. The walls were double layered sheet metal. Pink insulation filled cracks around a grimy window and a portable space heater hummed dangerously close to shorting itself out.

Kelly looked at me with casual indifference. "Two guys

break into my shop, smash up a bunch of stuff and you appear out of nowhere and try to fend them off. Only you get your ass kicked so bad you wake up as blue as a sunny afternoon."

"You don't make it sound heroic. They had a crowbar. And a pipe wrench. And there were *two* of them."

"The two guys who beat you up, you must have noticed something. Were they big, small? Any distinguishing marks? Did they *say* anything?"

"I think they worked for somebody. They said I didn't know who I was messing with."

"That's not helpful, you realize that, right? They give you a name?"

"No."

"They say their own names?"

"No."

"Did you learn *anything*?"

I wanted to punch him in the face. I had been out of prison six hours, awake almost thirty hours and I was tired as hell. In prison I thought I had taken care of myself. I worked out, I ate right, but I hadn't planned on fighting two junkies in the middle of the night while damn near frozen to death.

"They were junkies," I said. "Had to be. I hit one hard enough to put him in the infirmary. His buddy must have dragged him out of here."

"He did. There's a trail of blood across the floor."

"Do *you* know who they were?"

He ignored me. Instead, he asked, "What time did you get here this morning?"

"Six, I think."

"It was twenty degrees out. Were you planning on waiting outside until you froze to death?"

I stared at him. I considered climbing over the table and

kicking his ass and he saw it in my eyes. He sat forward. Stocky and compact he had meaty arms and a short haircut. I might do it, his look said, but I would pay dearly for the pleasure.

He waited. I waited. I took a deep breath and let it go. He sat back and crossed his hands on his chest.

"A lot has happened in the last twelve hours," I said. "I didn't think about it."

"Why didn't Munroe bring you himself?"

"I don't know. We're not besties."

He sat forward, drummed his fingers on the desk, glanced at the phone, then back at me. "He said you did a twelve-year stretch, that you didn't kill the guy you went away for."

"I killed the guy," I said. "There was a paperwork mistake."

Kelly's eyes narrowed and he stared at me for a long minute. "You're telling the truth."

I didn't say anything.

"Do you know why he asked me to hire you?"

I looked around the office. "You need the help."

"No, I don't. I need a maid, not a mechanic. I already have a mechanic. He shows up on time and does good work. No, you're here because Munroe is a good cop. And a smart cop. He's trying to do two things at once."

"How long you known him?"

"Longer than I've known you."

"Why am I here?"

"Because Munroe thinks he owes me and maybe, in a way, he does. He's worried about all the business I'm losing."

"Those guys last night. They weren't the first."

"The third time. I don't know who they are. The first time, I thought kids, after that, I knew somebody was trying to put me out of business."

"I'm supposed to be muscle?"

"We know how that worked. No, there's something else."

"You going to file a police report? Make some kind of statement?"

Kelly leaned back in his chair and looked up at the ceiling. "I'm not going to squawk about my troubles. Cops in this part of town don't care for paperwork if they can write at all. They tend to frown on the populace bringing them detective work. You saw the place as you came in. Believe it when I say it doesn't get much better when the sun comes up, freezing cold or not."

"Could you get any help from Munroe?"

"His answer was you."

"Good start," I said.

Kelly frowned. "I don't know what Munroe was thinking."

"Thanks."

"If he's got a plan, I'm not seeing it."

"Why don't you tell me the truth. Those guys worked for somebody. That somebody didn't hire them to hit this place at random. You know who's behind this or you got ideas. You piss off the wrong person? You owe them money?"

I watched him. Lou Kelly was a thick man. He wore a military issue green shirt with a black vest over it. The room was barely above sixty degrees but for him it could have been the middle of summer. They had names for men like him: pit bull, stocky, squat. This was a good physical description; it didn't capture his whole person. For one, his voice was too low and he spoke too slowly. And when I asked that question, he seemed to deflate, to become small.

"I don't have an answer for you," he said, staring me straight in the eyes. "Until I talk to Munroe, I've got nothing more for you."

"Those guys weren't exactly professionals, but they had a

purpose in coming here. They weren't after money. If they had, they would have come to you directly. They came to damage the place, smash up the cars. The damage is minimal but the loss of clients is huge. People won't come if they're worried their cars will get damaged."

"You've got it wrong."

"Do I? This isn't an issue of debt. This is an issue of property. Somebody wants it. Who?"

"That's not it."

"Maybe you hired those guys yourself. Maybe you're working an insurance angle. Planning for retirement?"

Kelly stood up. The pit bull was back.

"I built this place with my own hands and I'll be damned if I let you talk that way to me. This place is mine, whatever the hell's left of it, and I stand behind everything I've ever done. I've worked hard and did right by people. You spilled some blood for it, and to that I say thanks, but it's siphoned off gallons of mine."

He came around the desk. I remained seated.

"You, a killer, judging me. I spent the last twenty years working every day while you sat in prison. I created something here. I haven't destroyed anything. I *won't* have you talking to me that way."

"I'm sorry," I said. "I wasn't trying to insult you. I'm asking questions is all."

He looked down at himself, at his posture, blinked and turned back to his chair. He took several deep breathes and sat down.

"Do I get the job?" I asked.

Kelly snorted. "You're a god damn piece of work, Brogan, you really are."

I grinned at him.

"You may think I'm doing you a favor giving you a job,

but the truth is there's no money here, the work has dried up."

"I figured as much coming in."

"Let's focus on the guys from last night."

I told him every detail I could but it wasn't much. When I finished, he shook his head. "I don't know anyone like that."

"It's unlikely you would," I said. "Hiring a couple of junkies makes sense for this kind of job. They make money smashing the place up, and steal what they can and sell it for drugs. A double win in their eyes. And if you had cameras or a witness, it would be easy to dismiss them as just that, thieving druggies. No sign of a bigger plan. This being the third time, though, changes things for us."

"I don't want any cops."

"Not even Munroe?"

"Not even Munroe."

I nodded. "The situation this morning, it didn't happen as far as the cops are concerned, but that doesn't mean it didn't happen."

"Something like that," Kelly said.

"What do we do now?"

Kelly reached in to the upper left drawer of his desk and pulled out a small metal box. He fiddled with the lock until the top popped open, came out with a handful of small bills and handed me the stack. I didn't count them, just stuffed them in my pocket. He frowned at me.

It was the second time in as many days that somebody handed me a stack of money. It was getting to be a habit that made me uncomfortable. Eventually I'd have to pay it back.

"Find a store. Get some new clothes and shoes. You smell like a damn convict."

I stood up to leave when a dog came in through the doorway from the mechanic's bay. It was a big gray monster that stood with its back about even with my stomach. It had a square head and two big eyes that watched me warily as it strolled passed. It went to Kelly and he petted it. Once the animal was satisfied, it turned around a couple of times in front of the space heater and ended up in a ball about half as big as you'd expect.

"Nice dog," I said.

"He's purebred. Worth more than you."

"I'll keep that in mind."

"Those guys from this morning, they didn't scare you?"

"I didn't think about it."

"I was afraid you'd say that. Be here in the morning at eight. No earlier."

The dog turned over with its belly up to the heat and began to snore.

"Life's rough around here," I said.

"For some maybe, not for others."

FIVE

The nearest place with a decent bed and a hot shower was a low rent joint called the Sunshine Motel. Kelly gave me the address and I gave it to a cabbie who dropped me off after a five-minute ride. The motel was a two-story building with thirteen units on each floor. Trash littered the parking lot and a hunched Mexican woman pushed a cleaning cart between two units on the second floor. She glanced indifferently in my direction and returned to her work.

I stepped up to the glass window dividing me from the motel manager and asked for a room for a week. The manager, a skinny guy with scratched glasses, eyed me wearily. "You don't have any bags."

I pulled out my wad of cash and said, "Do you want to discuss my travel arrangements or make some money?"

He took the money and gave me a key to a room on the second floor.

Instead of going to the room, I walked across the street to a thrift store and bought a few days' worth of clothes. The lady behind the counter put it all in a big white bag and I carried it back to the motel room. Once inside, I dropped the bag on the floor, stripped down and said good night to the four empty walls.

I didn't know what time it was when I woke. This wasn't the kind of place that offered bedside alarm clocks. Maybe most people paid by the hour.

I climbed out of the bed and went into the bathroom for a shower. The water was hot and the pressure was good. Better than I had in prison and with more privacy. I stood under the water for almost twenty minutes. No limit, no schedule. I would have stood there longer but a rotten smell hit my nose. The kind of stench that stops you from being able to talk because you're gagging.

I turned off the water and stepped onto the tile floor. The cold tightened my body. The stench was worse. I still couldn't place it but it was familiar.

I tossed on a clean pair of pants and walked into the next room.

Roy Adler sat in a chair at the round table next to the door. He dangled a cheap cigarette out the window, his hand limp and his eyes watery. The smoke clogged up the air like a urine soaked ashtray. "Hello, Johnny."

"Thought I smelled your brand of sewer," I said.

Adler's face was framed in shadow. He had eyes that hadn't relaxed in a long time. Sharp cheekbones pulled his gray skin tight, giving his wide forehead a shiny wet look. His suit needed pressing, and the cigarette danced like a sparkler in the low light, ash falling onto his coat and the floor. He took a drag and flicked the butt through the window. "You never did like my brand."

I finished dressing: white t-shirt, blue flannel shirt, and heavy wool socks. I put on a pair of leather work boots a size too large. The socks made them comfortable.

31

"Close the window," I said.

He scowled at me and tried to close the window. He pushed down on one side and then the other, not quite getting either side to go down right. He shot me a sour look and gave the window the best shove he could, but left a good half foot gap.

"What are you doing here?" I asked.

"The door was unlocked. Thought you wouldn't mind."

"You need to leave now."

"Oh, come on, Johnny. It's been a long time! I came—I came to see how you're doing."

"I didn't die on the inside like you said I would."

Adler's mouth parted in a nasty shape that matched the crazy in his eyes. "Funny thing that. I was young, you know. Angry and all that. I am glad you got out. I mean, I don't wish nobody no harm. Life's precious and crap."

I put on my coat.

Adler stood up and barked, "Why'd you come back? I mean, you could have gone anywhere—you should have gone anywhere. Not here. This isn't your home anymore."

He pointed his finger at me, waving it accusingly. A head shorter than me, he wasn't as thick as I remembered. A few years older, he'd always been bigger than me in high school, but now he was stooped and thinner. He was a coat hanger in a suit. I noticed the gun hanging off his belt in a holster next to a badge.

"How long you been a cop, junkie?"

He pulled his suit coat wider, hooked his thumbs into his belt and pulled it up so the badge rose and fell. A detective badge. Real tough guy stuff. "I'm legal, Johnny. I can kick the living shit out of you if I want and you can't do a thing about it."

I walked up to him and looked down into his eyes. "Are

you sure?"

He stepped back a foot, bumped into the table and wiped his nose on his sleeve. "You're a real prick, Johnny, a real prick."

"Why are you here?"

"We're old friends. I'm here to congratulate you. You got out. That's great."

"*Why are you here?*"

He collapsed into the chair. "You shouldn't have come back. It's not like before. It's not like it was when we were kids."

"What are you talking about?"

"The city isn't safe anymore, if it ever was. You do things, you lose yourself. Everything goes rotten."

"You're not making any sense."

"They're going to kill you, you know, right? They got you out for a reason. Munroe, he's in on it. He's one of them. Why you think it was so easy you getting out?"

"You wanted me dead. Sounds like you'll get what you want."

He slumped down in the chair and fumbled around for a cigarette. He pulled one absently from the pack and let it sit unlit between two yellowed fingers.

"How did you know I was here?"

"I'm a cop. Finding people is easy in this town. You don't have much money. There's only so many places you could hide."

"I'm not hiding."

"Well, you should, damn it! When your name came up on the docket, I knew something was up. You had a twenty year stretch ahead of you. The whole thing was crazy from the start. And now this? The Russian giving himself up, admitting to killing Egorov's brother? That was just plain crazy. You didn't do it. Who would have thought?"

"You know I killed him. I've never denied it."

He laughed. The laughter caused him to cough a harsh braying sound. "You're funny, Johnny. You're the only con I know who admits to killing a man. Every other killer I know does his damnedest to lie about it, but you, you probably been telling everybody the truth and they ignore you, don't they? I bet you told the cops when you got out that you killed Egorov and they ignored you. You got some kind of luck!"

"It was self-defense."

"Right. I got it. I understand. That guy—that guy did it. He said so. Everybody knows it. They had the trial and they let you go. You got vindicated, man. You're free. You're *not* a killer. Record's clean. They got the right guy now. Perfect world."

Roy Adler made me sick. He wasn't worth the cost of rehab. He needed to crawl into a gutter and die. Being a cop just made it worse. Any decent police force should have taken one look at him and tossed him out on the street.

"Where's your sister?" I asked.

"What? What are you talking about?"

I grabbed his lapels and lifted him. I misjudged his weight and pulled him faster and harder than I expected. He was horribly light; bones held together by a cheap suit. He shook with fear.

"Where's Charlie?"

"I haven't seen her in years! Honest. She hit the big time, left me behind. Just blew me off. Called me a junkie and an anchor. An anchor, man! I gave her everything. She had inside information!"

"You need to leave now."

"You gotta understand. I'm trying to help you, Johnny. OK? OK? We both know it was a con job, you getting out. It was the only way Petr could get direct access to you. But you have to appreciate the effort, you know? That was slick work what they did."

"What's your point?"

"The whole damn department is running wild thinking maybe they got a chance at catching him. They think he's a genie in a bottle, going to grant him their three wishes. But you can't catch a guy like that, not when he's got that much power. You know, right?"

"Not everybody thinks that way."

"Jesus, Johnny, you killed his brother! Russians, they don't take that lightly, not at all. I'm surprised they didn't kill you on the inside."

"They tried."

"You're crazy. You should have run. You should have never come back. You should go up in the mountains, hide among the tree people. We've been keeping tabs on Egorov for years. He's got more guns and cocaine and people than his brother ever had. Nobody can touch him. He runs the entire city from Russia. And now he's coming for *you*. He's going to bring a lot of guns and a lot of death, Johnny."

"How much time do I have?"

"What?"

"How long before Egorov arrives?"

"I don't know, honest I don't. They never tell me anything, you know."

He stared at me, his mouth open, his jaw moving trying to undo what he had just said.

"Go home, Roy."

"Sure," Adler said. His face was sweaty now. His eyes blurry. "Sure, I should go home. Try to get some sleep. That'd be nice, sleep. Terry, she tells me that all the time. I don't sleep enough. I got married. Did I tell you? Eight years

35

now. She has a daughter we're raising together. I'm an actual father."

I opened the door. Adler sat in the chair staring at his unlit cigarette. He had mashed it between his fingers until it snapped in two. Tobacco stuck out of both ends.

"Sure," he repeated. He stood up. He leaned on the table, the cigarette tumbled forgotten to the floor. "It's time I go home. I need to go."

SIX

It was well after midnight. I left the motel room and walked the empty streets with no thought of where I was or where I was going. Gray mist clung to the tops of the buildings obscuring the glistening halos of what little light remained in the city. The new coat was warm and blocked the wind. The boots pushed through the snow like plows.

I was *free*: no more walls, no more restrictions. I walked. I passed closed businesses, snowbound parks and homes with darkened windows. Walking by the river, I paused and watched the black waters cut through the ice.

After several hours, I thought of food, but the shops I passed were closed, some of them permanently. I had to walk another mile before finding an all-night diner standing on a lonely corner, the open sign fuzzy through the snowfall. Big glass windows, shiny chrome and the smell of sizzling hamburger made my stomach rumble. Two men huddled outside the entrance smoking and shivering in coats that belonged to summer. They nodded and I nodded back. I stepped inside. The heat stung my face but I grinned anyway.

I was starving.

I counted six customers, four singles and one couple, spread out across high backed plastic booths. Fresh coffee sat before two empty seats at the counter. Two heads bothered to turn my direction, but once they got their fill, they turned back to their own business. After the cold walk, the restaurant felt uncomfortably hot. I took off my coat and hung it on a hook next to a booth. I sat down facing the door.

A pint-sized waitress with black hair pulled into a tail said, "Just a minute" as she moved around the room filling coffee cups. I didn't mind waiting. She was enjoyable to watch. She had a lively step I hadn't expected from a waitress working the graveyard shift. When I realized I had this idea that all waitresses working the midnight shift were old, worn and pug faced, I laughed.

"What's so funny?" she asked, appearing and pouring coffee at my nod.

"Laughing at my own expectations," I said.

The coffee smelled good. She smelled better.

"Menus are there. Order when you're ready."

She moved away and I watched her go.

The menus were thick cardboard held together with metal rings. I found what I wanted on the second page, slipped the menu back in the holder and waited for the waitress to return. When she came around again, I said, "Steak. The biggest you got and yams and green beans."

She laughed. "Yams? You're kidding, right? You mean like sweet potatoes? I can tell you straight up there isn't a yam in this place. You can go search the kitchen if you want."

I looked at her name tag. "Well, Sam, no yams or sweet potatoes. What else you got?"

"We have mashed potatoes. I'm *supposed* to tell you we peel them fresh in the morning, but they're powder and we make

38

them with water instead of milk. Want some of those?"

"I'll pass."

"Me, too. I don't eat from a box if I can help it. Now the steak is good. We get decent cuts from a butcher just up the street. And the beans they can't make dehydrated so they're not bad. You want steak and beans?"

"Yes, please."

"Anything else to drink? We have beer on tap. Nothing spectacular but it is cold."

"Sold."

She left to fill the order, and I sat back in the booth enjoying the cushion. In prison, you get plastic. A lot of plastic and a lot of concrete.

At the end of the table a miniature jukebox automatically flipped through pages of songs I didn't recognize. I enjoyed looking at the titles and the album artwork until Sam came back with the beer.

"Don't put money in that thing, it hasn't worked in years," she said.

I thanked her. She left and I turned to my beer. Tiny bubbles traced crooked lines on their way to the white foam head. My hand shook as I picked up the beer and brought it up to my lips. My head spun as the mouthful burned my tongue. After the first two sips, I gulped the rest down and waved Sam over for another one.

"Are you going to be trouble?" she asked.

"Nothing but a paying customer. One more and that's it. The beer's just too good to be true."

"Mister, that beer is piss and water. Now if you want something—"

"It was fine," I said. "One more and that will be it."

"Sure thing."

She came back with another beer and I took my time

nursing it. I caught her watching me and by the time she brought my steak around she appeared satisfied I wouldn't get drunk and tear up her diner.

I didn't waste time chatting her up. She put the plate in front of me and I dug in. For the next ten minutes, nothing else in the world mattered. That cheap diner meal was the best food I'd had in twelve years.

When the plate was clean, she stopped by. "Do they not have steak where you're from?"

"Not like that," I said.

I paid the bill, and she hesitated just a second before taking the money and walking back to the counter. One of the smokers left the diner along with a few of the other folks. A clock over the counter said it was after four a.m. and like most of these folks I had a job to get to in the morning. The idea felt funny, like wearing somebody else's shoes. I was looking forward to the work, but it felt like a life belonging to another man. And maybe it did. The smart thing to do was head back to the motel room and sleep, but I knew it wouldn't happen. I was a free man now and for a couple of hours I didn't want any rules.

Out of the corner of my eye I saw Sam buried in a heavy winter coat pass by the man at the counter. She stared ahead, not noticing his greedy look. Or maybe she noticed and chose not to acknowledge it. Be calm and don't give the beast a reason to pounce was a kind of defense.

She opened the front door letting in cold air. She turned left, passing by my window, but I couldn't see her face through the frost. The man at the counter finished the last of his coffee, stood up and placed a few bills on the counter. He drifted: put his coat on, checked his hat, walked outside. He turned left, passing by my window.

The steak churned in my gut. A nasty world we lived in;

lots of bitter pain and it was about to get uglier.

SEVEN

I counted to ten, stood up, tossed my jacket on, walked to the door and pushed it open so hard it slammed into the wall and knocked the *No Smoking* sign loose.

Somebody yelled from the counter, "What's the idea, buddy?"

"Call for an ambulance," I said, not looking back.

I turned left, passed by my empty booth, walked around the side of the building.

The parking lot had eight slots, five of them empty. Two cars sat at this end, both covered in today's snow. The last sat at the end, the drive-up tracks visible. A streetlamp at the end of the lot cast long shadows.

Sam stood near the far car facing the man. She asked him what he wanted, but he said nothing as he shoved her to the ground hard enough for her to cry out. She fumbled with her purse, but he knocked it away spilling the contents across the snow. His hands, big as frying pans, scooped up a pile of her hair and used it to pull her into a sitting position. She didn't wait. She climbed to her feet, tore off her glove and gouged at his face with her nails. He hit her with an offhanded blow intended more to stop her than hurt her. She stumbled to one side; her hat cockeyed, her hand pressed against her face.

That was enough.

At a full run, I hit the center of his spine with everything I had. He spilled forward onto the ground. I tumbled on top of him, pain numbing my arm. All I got from him was a grunt.

Sam kicked his face with her snow boot. His head snapped back. I heard the scream and the pop of cartilage at the same time. He brought his hands up as she kicked again. He caught her foot and twisted her. She cried out under the strain and rolled to her side to release the pressure. He punched her once in the side. She went still.

I dropped my elbow down on the back of his neck and heard a satisfying crack. I got one more punch across the side of his face from behind because he turned around slow like an ocean tanker. He swung hard twice. The first blow landing in my gut, the other hit my cheek. I saw stars, my vision faded and I stumbled to my knees.

The bandage on my head split open and blood dripped from the wound. I watched it melt the snow and disappear into the hole.

I took a deep breath. A second fight in as many days, but I wasn't going down this time. I had to be smarter than just throwing punches. This guy, I couldn't go toe to toe with and win. I had to think.

I leaned forward to take deeper breaths and try to clear my head. He must have thought I was out of the fight because he turned towards Sam. Rising, I kicked the back of his knee hard. He fell backwards, hit the snow on his back and stared up at me in confusion. I brought my boot down on his jaw. It snapped. His eyes bulged wide and fluttered momentarily before shock shut his brain down.

Sam sat up, clumps of snow in her hair. She climbed to her feet, walked over to the man and without hesitation stomped her foot down on his chest. He didn't react; he was out. The print looked tiny on the wide expanse of his coat.

I stepped between her and the man. "It's over. Any more and you'll just break your foot."

She turned away, her big blue eyes misty.

"Let's get back inside," I said. "We can talk to the cops in there."

"No cops," she said.

She ignored me when I asked her why. She picked up the scattered items of her purse like each was a family heirloom. I tried to help but she pushed me away. I stepped back. When she had gathered the contents, she stood and took a deep breath. She appeared calm and the color was back in her face. She held something up in the light I couldn't see. Seeing my lack of understanding, she said, "Pepper spray. I couldn't get it out fast enough. I never had a chance, did I?"

I didn't answer her. She would have needed a lot of luck in the cold with gloves on and against a larger opponent already on top of her.

"I can't find my keys. I can't find my *damn* keys. Can you help, please?"

Her voice was a whisper, childish in its questioning. I was astonished at the change. She must have seen it.

"I'm fine," she said. "Just—just need a minute to collect myself. It's—it's no big deal, OK? I can handle it. The keys, they're on a blue ring."

We walked in a slowly expanding circle, both of us staring at the ground and sifting snow. I walked by the guy lying on the ground in the same position we'd left him. I kicked him in the shoulder. "Hey," I said. "Where's the lady's keys?"

He mumbled through thick wheezing breaths but the words made little sense. He wouldn't be talking right for a long time with a busted jaw. I kicked him again, this time harder. He rolled over, his face the greasy white of undercooked pork chops. His irises were pinpoints almost invisible in the low light. His head slumped and he used the snow as a pillow.

"He doesn't have them," I said.

I continued searching but found nothing.

A woman in her fifties wearing the same uniform as Sam appeared around the corner of the restaurant. She clutched her arms around herself shivering and appearing about as brave as a mouse. "What's going on out here?"

The way she said it sounded like she already had an opinion. Either everything was fine and she could run back into the warmth or she would have to stand before a judge self-righteously talking about how she'd found me standing over a man I had brutally murdered. Her look said she was hoping for the latter.

"Did you call the ambulance like I told you?"

The woman used her arms to push her breasts higher, and I wondered if she was about to pull out a frying pan or a rolling pin. "Did you hurt that man?"

"Go make the call before this monkey freezes to death."

She peered quietly at the man on the ground but gasped when she saw Sam standing behind me. "Are you all right? Did this guy—"

"Does it look like I hurt her? Maybe we all just slipped on the ice."

The woman ran to Sam and inspected her head, her cheek and her arms. At one point, she clucked her tongue.

When I turned to leave, Sam touched my arm. I turned back and found her smiling. Even wearing a thick winter coat, she looked tiny.

"It's OK," Sam said, looking into my eyes. "This man helped me."

I wanted to pick her up, hold her in my arms till we both couldn't breathe any longer.

The waitress squinted at me. "What's your name?"

"Johnny Brogan," I said.

Sam repeated it under her breath and I wanted her to say it again.

"Thanks for your help," I said, facing Sam. "You got in several good hits too."

Sam blushed. I smiled at her. The waitress clucked again.

"What do you want?" I asked the waitress. "Going to whack me with a rolling pin?"

Her eyes narrowed and for a second I thought she would produce a rolling pin, but she only said, "Sam, let's go back inside. I'll call a cab for you."

"It's OK. I'm too worked up. Walking home will help me unwind."

"You sure? You don't want to press charges against this *thing*?"

Sam looked down at the man. "No, he got what he deserved."

"Suit yourself. Here, you left these on the counter. I came out to give them to you."

She handed Sam a set of keys on a blue ring.

Sam turned to me. "Will you walk me home?"

I nodded.

We were walking away when the waitress said, "I'll have Howie take care of this guy."

The way she said it, I knew Howie was the kind of guy I'd

buy a drink.

EIGHT

We walked in silence for several blocks. The air was bitter and the ground thick with black ice. Sam nearly fell once, but I caught her and for the effort I got a smile and a squeezed hand. I didn't ask how far we had to walk. She could have led me around all day. At a street corner she stopped and looked up at me. Even in the cold her face was soft, gentle, and warm. I wanted to caress it.

"Thank you for your help, Johnny."

Looking into her eyes, I realized I knew nothing about this woman and I didn't need to. Maybe that made me the biggest fool in the world but it didn't bother me. Beautiful and tiny she calmed me in a way I hadn't ever felt.

"Johnny Brogan," she whispered. "I like saying your name. *Johnny Brogan*." She took a deep breath and let it out slow. "It's been a long time since anybody's done something nice for me, Johnny. A real long time."

I noticed creases around her eyes, tiny lines of worry. A small touch of dark eyeliner highlighted her blue irises. She had a haunted distance in her eyes like she couldn't dream anymore. She danced nervously from one foot to the other, moving like a fighter always working to avoid the next punch. Wherever she'd come from, whatever had brought her to working a dive in a lousy part of town, it hadn't taken away her nervous hope.

"You did a good job holding your own back there," I said.

She laughed, her breath's warmth puffing into the air. "You did most of the heavy work. Is that something you do often, jump into other people's business?"

"Been a long time since I made my own decisions. But I think I did right."

Her eyes lowered when she spoke next, so much so I had to lean in to hear her. "How long were you in prison?"

"I didn't say anything about prison."

She shrugged. "You were gone a long time, you said, it wasn't the military. They have beer. And you've got an energy about you, like a kid facing the world for the first time."

"Twelve years. I got out yesterday."

"And this is your second fight already? You didn't start this one. Did you start the other one?"

"No. A couple guys tore up my employer's business, so I tried to stop them. It didn't end well for me."

"You're just out of prison and already employed? What do you do?"

"Mechanic," I said. "Worked on the transport buses. They were always breaking down. Took a lot of ingenuity to keep them running."

"You sound like you enjoyed prison."

"Better than staring at the walls of my cell. And it was honest work making something broken work again."

We continued walking. At the next block, she turned us right and her pace slowed.

"I didn't enjoy prison. The hallways were too narrow, the ceilings too low. Nothing was soft: not your clothes, not your bed, not even your pillow. Everything you touched was rigid. It was inhuman, but I belonged there. I had a price to pay."

"I'm sorry you had to go through that, but you give me hope for humanity. You're not blaming anyone else. Do you know how unusual that is?"

I shrugged. "Blaming others is easy. I don't like that kind of talk. It's a nasty, lazy way of thinking."

She frowned, pushed her hands deep into her pockets. "People don't talk like that anymore, not honestly. They act like you're a damn fool for doing the right thing. It's not a nice world we live in, you know?"

"Why don't you move away? Have to be places better than here."

Her laugh was gentle but sad. "I used to look at the bus schedules, but they don't go anywhere you won't end up dead for a dime. The good people left the city. I don't know where they went—maybe they never existed. I think it's a kind of hell being alone."

"I can help with that last part."

She laughed and grabbed my arm. "Come on, let's walk."

We walked several blocks in silence, then I asked, "You walk this far to work?"

"My car broke down and no buses run along this route this late, so I have to walk."

"What's the matter with your car?"

"I think it's the starter. A coworker looked at it, but he was more interested in me than the car."

"I don't blame him. I take it he knew nothing about engines."

"Not a lick. But he spent four hours under the hood. Finally, he gave up, but I made him dinner for the effort."

"And if I can fix it?"

She stopped and tilted her head at me. I wanted to touch her cheek but didn't. Instead I watched her eyes under the moon, bright and searching, looking to answer her own question. She took my hands into her own. It made hers look tiny. After a minute, she smiled and said, "I'd make you pancakes in the morning."

I said nothing. My body tensed, that muscle in the back of my throat cut off the air. She smiled at me, her eyes twinkling. Then she turned and pulled me further down the block. At the corner, she said, "This is it."

It turned out to be a single-story house with two wide windows on either side of a brown door. The trim was blue, the paint beige. Ugly colors, but it appeared well-tended as far as I could tell under the moonlight.

She grabbed the lapels of my coat and bit her lip. She was as old as me but she acted giddy like a school girl and I was doing all I could not to grab her up in my arms and press her lips to mine. "I don't want to be alone tonight—not after what happened. I've been teasing and I shouldn't. If you want to sleep on the couch, you can. I understand if you don't. It's an old couch and will give you back pain but…I'd like you to stay."

"Yes," I said.

She stood chest high, her face enveloped by the oversized coat, cheeks flushed from the cold, but she looked directly at me; no intimidation, no fear, just a newfound serenity gathered from one early morning walk. Her eyes misted, and she did a dancing skip, turned and rushed us inside.

Her house had a single bedroom, a good-sized kitchen and a living room big enough for a fake palm tree which covered most of the patio door. The furniture was secondhand and faded in places but patched together well. A pile of books about faraway places rested under the palm tree. A television the size of a basketball sat on the edge of a bookshelf filled with more travel books.

"My home," she said. "There's beer in the kitchen. Grab one and make yourself comfortable. I need a shower. I don't feel so well."

"I understand."

She closed and locked the bedroom door.

I stood in the kitchen and washed the blood from my hands and used a dish towel on my jacket. Overall, it wasn't much of an improvement. I touched my face and flinched. It would be ground beef for several weeks. I found my way to the couch with the beer, had about half and was drifting off to sleep when the bedroom door opened.

Sam appeared wearing shorts and a college jersey. "This is me," she said, smiling shyly.

I could have stared at her all night. Nothing about her was wrong; every bit was purely right. I nodded and whispered the words, "Thank you."

She nodded in return and then came forward frowning. "Ouch, your face. Damn, you're ugly in the light. Come into the kitchen. Here, get on your knees. Oh, no, I mean you're too tall. I can't reach your head."

I dropped to my knees on the kitchen floor. She messed around with my scalp, cutting bandage strips, applying gauze. Having her that close was distracting my brain in all kinds of ways. Her body was hard and tight and her breath came in shallow spurts and once I caught her looking at me, her eyes narrowing.

"You haven't been around women much."

"It's been a long time."

"There's a lot of tension coming off you."

"*Yeah.*"

"Well, you're in one piece."

"You keep your first aid kit in the kitchen?"

"It's where I draw the most blood. Let's go sit on the couch."

I followed her into the living room and sat on the couch in my previous place; she sat at arm's length, her legs hugged up under her.

"I wanted to move away," she said. "The city's been falling apart for a long time. I bought all those books thinking I could go to one of them. But I didn't. I couldn't leave. It's not because I want to stay, it's because these places are no different from here. Why run to the same place? You're not leaving your life behind. You're just changing the trees outside the window."

I drank more of the beer and set it down on the coffee table. I eased back into the couch. The low light made my eyes heavy. I yawned.

She lifted my arm and curled up under it. She felt soft and vulnerable and when she spoke her voice was quiet but unafraid. "I'm not looking for crazy fun tonight but I'm glad you're here. I want somebody…to hold me. It's been a long time. I feel safe with you. That means something, doesn't it?"

I squeezed her in my arm. She quivered; made a soft purring sound. She smelled damn good. I leaned in and inhaled deeply. She wiggled closer. Sensations I hadn't felt in a long time stirred in me but I let them go. I kicked off my shoes and put my feet up on the coffee table. She rested her head on my chest.

"I'm not even sure I like you," I said.

"You will by morning."

NINE

My stomach woke me with a sharp kick. I opened my eyes and smelled bacon. Sun streamed through thin curtains and beyond I could see a pine tree green as summer grass. In the kitchen, Sam made cooking sounds: metal on metal, running water and sizzling bacon. She hummed a song I didn't know.

I sat up and put my flannel shirt on. I had a feeling like living someone else's life.

I wasn't in prison.

The idea swam around in my head waiting for me to latch onto it to comprehend it. I wasn't ready. My hands felt the porous concrete walls of my prison cell. My nose smelled the unwashed inmates and sharp disinfectant wash used to clean the floors. My tongue tasted bland rehydrated eggs and oily preserved ham. My ears heard the deafening grate of closing metal doors.

Twelve years.

I shivered.

I stood slowly, brought myself back to now and walked into the kitchen. Sam stood over a cutting board, knife in hand, making strips of cheese with intent concentration. Her black hair curled down around her shoulder, long and silky, tied back with a thin strip of leather. She wore the same college jersey and shorts as last night. In this light, I had a better view of her long and muscular legs. I imagined touching them, their creamy softness caressed by my callused fingers, their tension quivering under my strength.

She danced around the kitchen light and happy, here a pause of hesitation, thought, consideration then a return to light movement and little sounds, a hum and an *aha*. This was the joy of being alive, a woman in her thirties, no longer awkwardly young, but strong, able, determined. Whatever years she'd lived, she'd lived them well, maybe rough, but nowhere in her did it say she'd given up.

She looked up. Smiled. "I'm not so shiny in sunlight."

"You're not, you're perfect."

I sat down at the kitchen table. All the aches came back and I groaned. My neck felt stiff and sprained and the muscles along my back spasmed protesting the movement. My face itched spread tight across bone. My eyes watered from the pins of light pricking the back of my skull. I leaned back in the seat and closed them.

I must have fallen asleep, because when I opened my eyes a plate of bacon, eggs and pancakes sat in front of me. Silverware and a crisp white napkin sat formally next to the plate. At the top of the spread was a huge glass of apple juice.

Sam sat next to me, her plate as fresh as mine. She reached out and gave my arm a squeeze. "Morning, Johnny."

"Morning, Beautiful."

"You look like hell."

"You look like heaven."

She blushed. I liked it. I tried to think of a dozen more

things to say but none of them made sense but it didn't matter. Everything was just fine sitting, eating with her there next to me. It was warm, intimate, comfortable.

She reached across the table and I watched as her breasts pressed against her jersey with clean lines showing her nakedness underneath. She took another bite. She liked to eat and I liked watching her eat.

"Less staring and more eating, please."

I grinned wolfishly and went back to my eggs and bacon. Much better than prison food and much better than diner food. I enjoyed the company and couldn't help myself grinning at her occasionally. She ate delicately, calmly, not like my usual company. I couldn't help but watch her, enthralled. She even put her fork down occasionally, which I never did in prison and didn't do now. I ate until my plate was empty and then waited patiently.

"There's three more pieces on the counter."

I ate the first piece before I sat back down. The next two I ate sitting while she watched. We smiled at one another when I was done.

"Thank you," I said. "I haven't ever had a breakfast like that."

"Did you taste it?"

"No. But it was good. I was hungry."

"I'll make you some pork chops later."

I smiled. "I'd like that. I'm also glad there will be a *later*."

"There will be, but in the meantime, we need to look at the car so I can get you to that job you say you have."

I stood up to clear the table, but she stopped me, laid her head and her hand against my chest. I put my arms around her and we stood like that for several minutes. Her eyes were closed and I could feel the tension in her body. It was a light, natural thing, a kind of energy that hadn't been there last night.

"It's a new day, Johnny. Things are possible."

We cleaned up the kitchen and afterwards she led me out to the garage. The car looked like hell; rusted side panels, a cracked windshield, a missing passenger side mirror, but for me it was what was under the hood that mattered. Sam handed me the keys and said, "It's nothing special, be lucky to get another ten thousand miles out of it."

I climbed behind the steering wheel, pressed in the clutch and tried turning over the engine. It made clicking sounds. Two more attempts brought the same result. I climbed out and popped the hood. A quick inspection told me nothing was particularly wrong. I was surprised to find a decent set of tools in the trunk.

"My father was an architect," she said. "He had tools for carpentry, for drafting, for the lawn, even for the kitchen. I sold all of them except those. He believed you should use the right tool for the job." She frowned. "He didn't get to teach me everything he knew. But I got most of it."

Something about the way she spoke made me leave it alone. It was her story; she'd tell it when and if she was ready.

"Do you have jumper cables? The battery doesn't have enough charge for the starter."

"I think my neighbor has some. I'll run over there."

She exited through a door that led outside and into the backyard. I leaned against the car while I waited. The garage contained enough space for two vehicles and a workbench. A dozen boxes filled the other space, each box labeled with large black letters: *COLLEGE*, *BASEMENT*, *CRAP*. A picture of Sam and an older man—her father, I guessed—hung over the workbench. They stood in front of the car I now leaned against, Sam smiling as bright as the fresh factory paint.

A car pulled into the driveway and Sam came through the side door with the jumper cables and a blast of cold air. "We can hook these up if we can push mine outside."

"If I'm wrong, we'll have to push it back in here."

She shrugged. "I've left it in worse places."

I opened the garage door. Cold air scraped my skin through the flannel shirt causing me to shiver. The houses were an arm's length apart, the driveways a single slab of concrete. Sam opened the neighbor's car door and popped the hood. I went around to the front of her car while she got behind the wheel and popped off the emergency brake. Once she had the car in neutral, I rocked it several times, gave it a good shove up and over the accumulated snow just outside the door.

Sam tapped the brake until the cars aligned, then popped the hood so I could apply the cables. Back in the house, she poured cups of coffee to warm us while the battery charged.

"You've had the car a long time."

"My father gave it to me when I graduated college. I never expected to have it this long."

I didn't ask about college, what happened afterwards, or why she was working graveyard at a dive. I said, "It looks like hell but the engine is solid. You change the oil and fill the tires, throw sandbags in the trunk, could easily last the rest of winter, maybe even a couple more winters."

"Cars are just cars. Good for taking you places and an occasional ride out of the city, nothing more."

I smiled. We didn't see cars in the same way. I saw the open road and freedom and that rumbling power under the hood when you get the right one. Maybe one day I'd get the chance to show her.

I set my coffee mug down, walked out to the car and sat in the driver's seat. The dash lights came on bright. I pressed in the clutch, turned the ignition and the engine turned over easily. I climbed from the car as Sam emerged from the house. She planted a kiss on my cheek.

"Thank you, thank you!"

"You know, you treat them good, they can be reliable."

Her eyes narrowed, and she said, "I guess I owe you some pork chops, don't I."

"Whole reason I'm here."

TEN

We rode in silence to Kelly's shop, both of us working through our own thoughts. The future didn't exist to me in prison, not in any concrete way. Plans, possibilities, they made me sick to my stomach, not because I wanted them but because I couldn't have them. I spent entire days angry, impotent, disillusioned and ready to snap at anyone in my way.

Riding along in Sam's car, watching children climb onto buses, old men cross streets, young girls dance through the slush, I realized I had a future. All those hopes, they could be real. I could think about them now. They were possible, but they scared me, every one of them except one: having Sam in my arms. I rested my hand on her leg while she drove. She squeezed my hand and turned back to driving with a smile.

I frowned. A beautiful woman, I could see her being part of my future. But not yet. I still had to face Petr Egorov and I had to do it alone. He couldn't find out about Sam because if he did he would use her against me. She needed to disappear.

"We're here," Sam said.

I opened my eyes. She'd parked the car in front of Kelly's shop. The engine was still running, heat trickling from the vents. I leaned over and kissed her. She returned it hesitantly. She bit her lip, pulled back and said, "We had a good evening. I appreciate that. But if you don't want to see me again, I understand."

"That's not it," I said.

"No games, please. Just be honest."

"There's things I need to consider, and a possibility that didn't exist yesterday. You're that possibility. I *want* to see you again. I *need* to see you again. The situation was simpler yesterday but it's better today."

She kissed me. This time with force. She pressed against me, her arms squeezing me, her body close and hard against me.

I climbed from the car and, watching her drive away, took a deep breath. The air felt fresh, new. The car turned and disappeared around a corner. I walked to the shop, the cold forgotten for the first time in a long time.

Kelly had done a manageable job with the door. The shavings were gone and the scratches remained, but he'd replaced the knob and added a steel deadbolt.

Inside I found a guy in overalls leaning over a Ford pickup. His head was under the hood so I knocked at a jerry can to get his attention and he obliged by popping his head out and grinning at me.

"Howdy!" he said.

He wasn't a kid anymore, but his face had all the youthful color and texture of a nineteen-year-old. He was big, damn big, taller than me and wider too. Something about the way he held himself said he wasn't used to his own size either. He was careful when he walked, like a man gets when he's

61

knocked over a few too many things and realized it's because of his size. And from the way his overalls pulled against his shoulders and arms, he was packing a good amount of muscle. I was glad it wasn't him I'd found in the garage the other night. But the way he grinned at me, I doubted I'd ever find him sneaking around a garage causing mischief.

He wiped his hand repeatedly until he was sure it was clean, then he thrust it at me like a club. "You must be Johnny Brogan."

"I am," I said, taking the club in my own hand. We shook and he grinned at me like I was his best friend.

"I'm Julian. Lou gave me this job working on cars six months ago. It's the best job I've ever had. Lou's a good guy."

He looked at me like I was supposed to agree with him so I did. Then he continued. "I wanted to thank you for helping out the other night. Lou didn't tell me what happened, but I saw the door and the damage. He was upset about the expense, but he appeared pleased. I think that's because of you. I think he likes you."

"He didn't mention that to me."

He nodded sagely. "He's over forty. Old people like him have trouble expressing their emotions. I like him, though. He's a good guy."

I smiled. "You mentioned that."

"And I like working here. Nobody gives guys like me a job, not anymore. I did felony time and I'm not so quick, so guys like me, they struggle. Lou helps me so I don't have to struggle so hard. He's a good guy, you understand?"

I said I did and then grinned. "We're on the same side, Julian."

"Good. Thank you."

He wiped the rag in his hand trying to figure out what to say next, so I asked, "What are you working on?"

He pointed at the car with the smashed windshield. "I replaced the timing belt already, and now I'm working on the spark plugs. Lou wants me to replace the windshield this afternoon. It's sad what those guys did. Because of them we won't make any money on this job. They smashed up the engine and the exterior good. I'll talk to the customer, see if they'll accept used parts where we can but they won't come back. Nobody does these days."

"Business is down?"

"Business is *dead*. It makes me sad. Can't be a mechanic if there's no cars to work on. Lou says business will pick up, but I struggle to believe him. I see the empty buildings around the neighborhood. Nobody comes to this part of town no more. Not since I started six months ago anyway."

"Yes," I said, "Six months ago."

I thought of the drive in with Sam. The street had two inches of snow and the sidewalks had not been cleared. I figured four inches of snow fell throughout the night. Not enough to shut the city down like the bus driver thought, but enough to roll up the welcome mats. Still, businesses don't like to close for any weather. It's a matter of pride to be able to say they provide their service the weather be damned and besides, there's always money to be made. Only Julian was correct; the money had left this part of town.

From his office, Kelly called us over. Julian took the chair grinning. I stood in the doorway. The space heater propped up in the corner glowed red, but I couldn't feel any heat.

An orange and dirty shoe box sat in the middle of Kelly's desk. Kelly pointed at it and then at Julian. Julian picked up the box with one hand like it was empty, but I figured he could lift an engine block with that same one hand.

"What is it?" I asked.

"Automobile parts."

"Where they going?"

"*Dunnam's Bar*. Julian knows the place."

I took a deep breath. "Why send both of us?"

Kelly sighed. "You're new so I'll talk slow for your first week. Those are parts and you need to deliver the parts."

"What's in the box?"

"I only know English so you're getting the message the only way I know how to say it: automobile parts."

"Why both of us?"

"What the hell's the matter with you? Get in the passenger seat of the truck and look out the damn window. That's all you need to do."

"Send Julian. He's got seniority."

Kelly stood, pulled himself to his full height and scowled at me. An old-school scrapper, even now, a toothless old lion, he wasn't tame. "*Both* of you go. *Both* of you. Deliver the damn parts and don't forget to write the mileage."

Julian followed me out to the bay. He wasn't grinning anymore.

ELEVEN

Julian climbed onto the driver's side and I took the passenger side of the bench seat. He'd tossed the box between us. The truck started with a belch of smoke and didn't push anything warm out of the vents until we were two miles down the highway. I figured Julian drove the speed limit because that was the truck's top speed.

"Do you want to open the box?" Julian asked.

"He ever do this before?"

He shook his head. "But the kid who normally makes the deliveries, he hasn't been around for weeks. I don't think he's coming back. Folks are leaving this part of town because there's not much in the way of paying jobs."

"Plenty of crime."

Julian nodded. "Too much crime. I seen people bar their windows and doors, don't talk to their neighbors anymore. Happened to Ashley once. She went to visit the neighbors, brought cake and everything, and they yelled at her through the door to go away. An elderly couple. They were scared."

I picked up the box and dumped the contents out on the

seat. Ten seconds passed while I let myself breathe. Then I swore, staring at a distributor cap and a bundle of wires.

"See," Julian said. "A distributor cap. Looks Japanese. What's the matter with you? Are you going to throw up? You're shaking."

"Drugs," I said.

"Are you on drugs? Should I take you to the emergency room? I'll have to tell Lou and he'll have to tell your parole officer. You'll go back to prison."

I set the box down and sunk into the old Ford's bench seat and closed my eyes. "I'm not on drugs."

"That's good," Julian said. "You don't want to do that stuff."

I laughed. "You're right."

"Lou said you killed someone over drugs. I'm sorry you were a drug dealer."

"I wasn't a drug dealer. I made deliveries like we're doing now. I thought I was delivering parts, only some of the packages contained cocaine."

Julian nodded. "Bad stuff. I see those guys around the clinics with their clothes all nasty and that look in their eyes. They smell horrible and their arms—they scare me."

"I didn't know about the drugs. I wanted to be a mechanic."

"Me too! I wanted to work on cars ever since I was a kid! Made a go-cart when I was twelve. Only one in the neighborhood."

"Back then the shops were run by the Russians, they fixed cars, but their real industry was drug trafficking. I didn't know about the drugs. They gave me a package and a destination and I delivered. No questions asked because I never thought to ask. I screwed up a delivery one day. They came after me and the situation got messy."

"That's wrong," Julian said. "That's just wrong."

"Probably," I said.

"So you thought Lou was making us to do the same thing? He's honest, Johnny, as honest as they come. I'm serious. I wouldn't work for him if he wasn't. We're all trying to stay clean these days."

"Stop at that gas station," I said. "I need water."

I bought a bottle of water from the attendant while Julian filled the gas tank. Then I stood near the pump watching the cars merge onto the highway. I followed them until they disappeared over the horizon.

"You ever think about running away?" I asked.

"All the time. Sometimes I get so worked up I want to hit the road and leave everything behind, even Ashley."

"The world feels too big."

Julian nodded. "It lasts about a month. Every direction you look it's like the world goes on forever. Those walls made us feel safe."

We got back in the truck and Julian wrote the mileage down on the gas receipt. The truck, already warm, started easy and didn't produce the black smoke cloud. Julian drove it slow back to the highway and merged into traffic.

"Why did you go to prison?" I asked.

I normally didn't ask the question. Whatever a guy did in the past, that belonged to him. Only, Julian didn't fit any pattern I could see. He didn't appear emotion driven and prone to the poor behavior that ended in prison sentences. And he talked about good and bad like he cared about it.

"I valeted at a hotel downtown on the weekends. This guy drove up in a Porsche 911. The car was amazing, had this silky gray paint that made it ripple in the light. Custom silver rims like I'd never seen before and worth more than I'd make in years. The car was beautiful." He frowned. "But the guy, he was a jerk. He tossed the keys at me like I was a punk. Just left me standing there like I was nobody, invisible. I watched him walk into the hotel with his girlfriend and I climbed behind the wheel and the second I heard the engine purring I knew what I would do. I hit the gas and tore on down the road straight to the highway."

He laughed, his hand tightening on the steering wheel. "The cops chased me for twenty miles on the Interstate. Then I tried to take an off ramp and missed, went flying a hundred feet into a ditch. Totaled the car. Spent three months in intensive care. They put all kinds of metal in me. Sometimes I dream I'm flying, blue sky all around me. Then I hit the telephone pole and wake up screaming. They said it messed up my brain but I don't feel different. Sometimes people watch me and I get the idea I should say something but I just grin at them." He grinned. "I can tell you I won't steal another car as long as I live."

"Do you have a driver's license?"

"Lou got me a permit to drive the truck during working hours. We even have insurance. I don't consider it a license but I guess it is. Just not a normal one."

"What do you do at home?"

"Ashley drives. But she's so bad I catch myself pressing on a gas pedal that don't exist. Other than that, she's the best girl ever. Understand, I'm clean, Johnny. I'm clean for her and the baby."

"You have a child?"

"Ash is four months pregnant. Going to be a girl."

"Congratulations."

The rest of the trip we rode in silence. Julian fiddled with the radio station, only occasionally staying on one song or another. I couldn't make sense of his preferences so I sat back in the seat and thought about the parts box.

Kelly could have fired me over the attitude, but if he wasn't clean it wouldn't have mattered. I wouldn't have stayed. He appeared to be a solid guy, but external pressure can change a person, especially when the bills stack up. He was a mean son of a bitch but I could put up with that. What I didn't understand was this game about the parts. I didn't get his angle. His approach made little sense.

We pulled into the driveway and Julian parked the truck like it was his own pride and joy and not some ten-year-old rust bucket needing retirement. I stepped from the truck and stomped my feet to put some warmth back in them. We stood in the empty parking lot of a strip club long past its best days. The club sat on the edge of the highway with its neon sign flung up to the sky like a hitchhiker's thumb. Gray snow covered the sidewalks. Leafless bushes divided the space between the parking lot and the highway, doing little to block the accumulated debris and snow. A gray canopy hanging limply over a set of double wide red doors flapped in the cold wind.

"Nice place," I said. "I know where to take my next date."

"We go around back," Julian said.

At a side door twenty feet from a dumpster, he knocked once and waited about three seconds before pushing the door open and walking in.

A small guy with cracked teeth and a sweat-stained dress shirt stood inside with his back to us. He hadn't heard the knocking because an obnoxiously lit jukebox blasted heavy techno music loud enough to drown out machine gun fire. But when he saw the morning light cut a streak across the hallway floor, he turned, shading his eyes and scowling.

"What you want?"

"Delivery for Feld," Julian yelled at him. "A box."

Six inches shorter than me and far shorter than Julian, he

tried to act like he was leaning in on us. "Yeah?"

Julian stepped forward with the box in his hands and I wondered if some convincing was going to take place. Maybe the box convinced him. Maybe Julian's overalls did. Or maybe it was two big guys he couldn't take without a gun. He just sneered and waved us to follow.

He led us down a hallway lined with tapped kegs and empty liquor boxes to a large room with a pool table in the center.

Another guy, this one even shorter than the first, leaned over the table and took a shot. He missed, frowned and glanced up at us. He said a few words, but nobody could hear him so the first guy waved at his ear and shook his head.

The pool player pressed a button on the jukebox, and the noise instantly disappeared, leaving a ringing sound in my ears.

"Who the hell are you?" he asked. My distorted hearing made him sound far away.

The first guy pointed a thumb at us as if that was required to identify who he was talking about. "They're here to see Feld."

"He ain't here."

"They got a box, Palermo."

Palermo set his stick on the table, careful not to disturb the balls. "They got a box. Well, what's in the damn box?"

"Parts," Julian said.

"Parts? What kind of parts?"

"Body parts," the first guy said. "What the hell you think they are? These guys work for Lou Kelly."

"You're mechanics? You look like you deliver pizzas. You deliver pizzas?" Palermo asked.

"We're moonlighting," I said.

Palermo scowled at me. Apparently, only he could tell

jokes. I pushed it anyway. "We're also first chair cellists. You should see us play. We toss pizzas in the air and play cello. A real hoot."

He blinked. He was off center now. If the script was his, he could follow it. He struggled with improvising. "You both can't be first chair," he said weakly.

"No shit," I said. "I didn't know. Do I look like I play the cello? Do I look like I deliver pizza? We're here to drop off a box of parts to a guy named Feld. You're not Feld so you don't matter. Where's Feld?"

Palermo blinked again, considering, struggling with what to do next. Julian fidgeted next to me. Even he moved faster than this guy. Palermo turned to the first guy who stood slightly behind Julian. First guy shrugged. I waited, relaxed. They'd figure it out eventually.

Palermo took a deep breath, waved at Julian to approach. "Give them here. Let me see."

Julian handed him the box, and he opened it, ruffling a fat finger through the pieces of cast metal. From his expression, I could tell he didn't know what they were.

"Car parts," he said. He looked at the first guy. "What's the boss want with car parts?"

The first guy shrugged. "What they for, these parts?"

"Carburetor," Julian said. "I'd say for an American model. Not sure though because I didn't look close at them."

He had said distributor cap and cables for a Japanese model in the truck. I suddenly didn't feel so relaxed, but he didn't signal me in any way. The two guys stood around the box like it contained rabid kittens, two guys unable to decide what it was all about.

Palermo tossed the box on the nearby desk and shrugged. He pulled a large wad of cash from his front pocket and peeled off several bills. "Whatever. How much?"

Julian shook his head. "We were told just to deliver."

Palermo stuffed the cash back in his pocket. "Then get the hell out of here. We're in the middle of a game."

The first guy followed us to the door. He said nothing and we wouldn't have heard him if he had because Palermo had turned the music back up. I did however hear the door being locked behind us as we stood outside.

"What was that all about?" I asked.

Julian shook his head. "Lou wanted us to deliver parts. We delivered parts."

He walked to the truck and started up the engine. I followed him moving slow, trying to think about why none of this made any sense.

I settled in the passenger seat and stared out the window. Back on the highway I said, "You didn't tell them the truth about the parts."

Julian's hand clutched at the steering wheel but he didn't answer.

"Wannabe mobsters don't know nothing about cars and don't know we're coming. What the hell is going on, Julian?"

"They knew nothing about the parts. They didn't know we were coming."

"You're repeating what I'm saying."

He shrugged.

"I think Feld would be just as surprised to see us if he had been there. Could have been an awkward situation."

Julian nodded.

"Why would Feld have a Japanese car? Guys like that go for the big flashy rides, the obnoxious boats, not little foreign cars that get lost in the crowd."

"Feld is powerful," Julian said. "People do things for him. All kinds of things."

Julian jammed through the six saved radio stations until he

found one he liked and I settled back in the seat unable to enjoy the view. Snow blanketed the houses and covered much of the trash, but still the variety of buildings overwhelmed me. So much movement, so much vitality, even for a city grinding to a halt. I closed my eyes and kept them that way until we pulled in to the shop.

"Want to get a drink after I give Lou the keys?"

"Sure, but I'll take the keys," I said. "Meet you out here."

Kelly didn't look up from his newspaper when I came in. I tossed the keys onto the newspaper and he scowled.

"You cocky son of a bitch," he said.

"Shut up and listen," I said. "The next time you get the idea to send me into an ambush, don't. You couldn't have played it better if you'd wanted me dead. They carry guns on their own turf. If something had gone wrong, they could have killed us easily and you would have been left with nothing."

His face filled with anger and I thought he would make a move, but he stared at me, calculating and then he deflated like an air filled roadside advertisement. It made me sad and then it made me angry. He was an old man and a tired man. And we lived in a world that could break a guy like him. He had made a bad play and he knew it, but what options did he have? The game was stacked against him and even if he got to win a hand or two nobody else played straight. Why should he?

"Was it them?" He asked.

"No."

"So why are you crying? Nothing happened."

"You're a lousy general. You don't send your troops in without arming them first."

"What the hell you talking about? This isn't a war."

"You know better than anyone what we're dealing with.

You pushed me into it so now tell me. Who else is in this game? It wasn't Feld and his men. Who else could it be?"

"Get the hell out of here."

"Who's next?"

"I don't know."

"You're lying."

"No, I'm not. I don't know yet. I got ideas but nothing certain. I'm trying to find out though."

"You tell me as soon as you know. You understand? I don't like surprises, not when guns are involved."

"Maybe tomorrow, Brogan."

"Tomorrow," I said and walked out of the office.

Julian sat behind the wheel of a little car covered in more rust than paint. I slid in the passenger side and said, "Thought you didn't have a license."

"Don't have insurance, either. Where you staying?"

"Sunshine Motel."

He nodded as if he knew the place. "It's a sad place with a stupid name. My house, I have an extra room, you want it. Nothing great but better than the Sunshine. Stupid, stupid name."

I thanked him, but said I'd keep where I was at for now.

He put the car into drive and asked, "Everything fine with Lou?"

"Christmas morning happy," I said.

TWELVE

Julian chose a bar between the Sunshine Motel and Kelly's shop, which was good because his car had no heat and by the time we walked into the bar my face was numb. We sat down and ordered beers and once we had them, he asked, "Did Lou set us up?"

"Yes," I said.

"Why would he do that? We could have been hurt."

"He's an old man in over his head. He doesn't know how to fight this kind of war and he doesn't have the energy for it even if he did. We'll be lucky if he keeps the shop open till spring."

Julian and I sat in a booth along the wall opposite the bar. Six people lined the bar, four of them wearing variations of denim and flannel. The last two, a man and woman, appeared dressed for a date. The five men watched the game playing on the television hanging over the bar while the woman smoked long cigarettes and drank from a glass with an umbrella in it. The place was quiet enough I could hear her nails tapping on the glass in boredom. The bartender seemed to notice this too, so he turned up the television to drown her out.

"What can we do about it?" Julian asked.

"We need to find the men who vandalized the shop. If it wasn't Feld, who else is a possibility?"

Julian pushed his beer around on the table. After a couple of minutes, he said, "I don't know about poking around. Maybe we should leave well enough alone."

"Why's that?"

"I was out of prison two months when I met Ashley. Nothing stuck. No job, no house, nothing. I met people I thought wanted to be my friend, but they either robbed me or wanted me to do bad things. Some I fought. I hurt one man so bad I was sure the police would put me back in prison. But nobody came and it made me sad. I was ready to go back to prison. I didn't understand people but I understood prison. I felt safe there. I didn't worry about work or a place to sleep, you know?"

I nodded.

"The way I saw it, just getting by was better than dying, but I was dying, no doubt about it. I had no money, no place to live. I checked change slots at laundromats because I'd found a five-dollar bill in a dryer once. One night Ashley saw me making my rounds and asked me how much I made in a day. We got to talking and for the first time in a long time I felt visible to another human being."

He took a sip of beer with a shaky hand. "I looked like hell, hadn't shaved in days, my clothes stank, but none of that scared her. I think I was more scared of her. I hadn't spoken to anyone in days. No drugs, nothing like that, I was just disconnected from people. Nobody saw me.

"I told her I was looking for dinner money and she said if I could clean up, she'd buy me dinner. I thought she was joking, playing a game to hurt me. Only she didn't. She got me cleaned up that night and we had a cheeseburger together. I never understood what she saw but she saw something. She saved me. She's a good person.

"The next day she helped me get the job at Lou's. She got me all dressed up, and I did a real interview with him. She let me stay at her place on her couch and eventually we went on a real date. Four months ago she got pregnant. I got to tell you, I was never more afraid in my life. In those first few hours I thought about running away to every faraway place I could think of, but she sat me down and we talked through the entire evening, and in the morning, we had a plan and I wasn't afraid no more. I haven't been afraid of anything since. I love that woman more than anything in this world. She made the impossible possible for me and I would do anything for her. In a few months, she won't be able to work and it'll be up to me to bring home dinner. She'll need me like I needed her and I can't let her down. That's what this job means. There's not much work left anywhere. If Lou goes, I go and so do my girls. I can't let that happen."

"I appreciate you telling me your story, but I don't understand *why* you're telling it. What are you *not* telling me?"

He took a gulp of his beer, unable to meet my eyes.

"What is it?"

"I guess I'm just trying to say, I don't want to kill anyone."

"Nobody is asking you to."

"But what those guys did, that's wrong. Something needs to happen to them. But I'm worried now. Before, I didn't care so much, but now I have something worth fighting for. I'm not afraid, I just don't want to get hurt."

"I care more about who hired them."

"There's no sense in it. Lou doesn't want to sell the shop.

He wants to be left alone so why can't they leave him alone? It's not right."

"Do you know who's pushing him around?"

"The only guy I've ever seen is Tancredi. He's a big guy, wears lots of jewelry and he never talks, just shouts everything. You could be two feet away from him and he shouts at you. I think he's deaf."

"When did you see him last?"

"He comes around occasionally. Lou is nice. He takes him into his office and they talk, only I can always hear what Tancredi is saying."

"What happens?"

"Tancredi makes Lou an offer, Lou refuses, Tancredi gets upset and leaves."

"Doesn't appear all that bad."

"It wasn't, not until recently. The last three times Tancredi showed up with several men. Big guys, the kind that hurt you until you don't get up again. They had their same talk and when it was done Tancredi threatened Lou. I was mad and started towards his office when one man came out and stopped me. Told me I could end up in the hospital if I didn't think this through. I'm a big guy but this guy was bigger. And he had a partner. Lou came out and made it all fine and they left. I guess they came back a couple more times, the last time I wasn't there, but Lou was pretty shook up."

"Did you learn why Tancredi wanted the place?"

"They never talked about it."

"Did he say how much he was offering?"

Julian told me.

I whistled. "That's a lot of retirement money. And Kelly wouldn't take it? There's stubborn and there's dumb. With that kind of money, he could have retired on the spot. What stops a guy from taking that kind of payout?"

"He doesn't want Tancredi's money, like it's tainted somehow. I think they started friends, but Tancredi got involved in a bad way and now Lou tolerates him. Lou's funny that way. He'll give you the shirt off his back unless you cross him. Then he won't even hold the door for you."

"He could take the money and never look back. All he has to do is not worry where it came from."

"Tancredi is involved with criminals. I think the big men who came with him the last couple of times were Russian."

"Russian?"

"They talked funny. Big, dark haired and tattooed. When they looked at me I got worried."

The waitress brought us another round of beers and we ordered burgers.

Julian asked, "Did you really kill someone?"

"A long time ago in self-defense."

"Lou said somebody else took responsibility."

"For a guy who doesn't talk about his own business, he likes talking about other people's."

"I overheard. Last week, before you arrived he talked with another man, a cop I think. They talked about you but I didn't know it was you. I didn't get too many details."

"You listen."

"I'm a bit slow but I'm not dumb. People forget that when I'm around."

"The cops set it up. They get the guy they want and they don't care much about the details."

"Sounds complicated."

"I've had easier weeks."

"You kill a man, someone else admits to it and the cops let you out of prison. Who admits to that?"

"Takes work, but a guy doing life could make bank claiming he did something he didn't do, if presented to the right interested party."

Julian considered. "Nobody offered me anything like that."

"Circumstances have to be right. A grain of truth has to make up the lie."

Julian sat back in the booth and waved his hands at me. "No way, I want nothing to do with it. No questions mean I know nothing. Right now, I like that. Sorry I asked."

The burgers came and we ate. Julian spent most of his time between bites eyeing me like he wanted to ask more questions, but eventually he gave up and focused on putting away his burger.

After the waitress took the plates, he said, "Tell me about the guys who jumped you. Maybe we can track them down, find out who they work for. It's probably Tancredi but it might not be."

"You a detective now?"

"Motivated. I want these guys."

"I thought you didn't want to get involved."

"I don't want to fight anyone but I can help in other ways. Maybe you can talk to them once we find them."

"Talk? That what you're telling yourself."

He sighed. "I don't want to lose Ash."

"I know."

I spent the next ten minutes answering his questions. He asked about their speech, the way they dressed, how big they were and whether I could point them out again if I saw them, which I figured wouldn't be a problem. I was impressed with his questions and said as much.

"Television," he said. "Can't read words anymore but I love the cop shows."

We finished the beers and when the check was paid, Julian said, "I'll see what I can do to find them. The guys you described don't sound like anybody Tancredi would know, but if they were drug users, like you said, they wouldn't be part of his regular crew. Tancredi tries to be the big-time businessman. I don't think he wants anything to do with drugs."

"You be careful," I said. "Asking questions about guys like this leads to trouble. Don't do it if there's any risk."

He laughed. "I can do it. I'm one of the good guys, right?"

THIRTEEN

At 2 a.m., I awoke to someone knocking at the motel room door. The knock sounded like an embarrassed neighbor asking for a cup of sugar, not a demand to throw on the nearest article of clothing and go scrambling for the door. I turned to sit on the side of the bed, yawned and rubbed my face. Wouldn't be the cops; they would be insistent. Wouldn't be the Russians; they wouldn't knock.

I tossed on a pair of pants and drew back the window curtain. Through the window frost I saw a slender woman wearing a thick coat huddled in the shadows. I thought it might be Sam but she didn't know about the motel.

I opened the door and let in the cold.

The woman leveled a gun at my chest and said, "Hello, Johnny."

"Hello, Charlie."

She wasn't the girl I fell in love with years ago. Makeup caked her nose and cheeks, but couldn't hide the effects of the cocaine. Her face, already too thin, wore a tight mask of insolence. Tiny white teeth poked out between bright red lips. A black fur coat hugged her hips and contrasted with the paleness of her legs. Long strands of black hair cascading around her shoulders gave her a childlike appearance. In her delicate hands the gun looked big, nasty and violent.

"Did you miss me?" she asked.

"Not for a minute."

"My brother's a cop. He can find people."

"I didn't ask."

"Are you going to let me in? It's cold out here and all I have is this coat."

"You're wearing boots."

"And a gun."

"It fits you."

The plastic hardness of her face cracked. "Please."

I stepped back, and she entered the room smelling of sex and expensive perfume. I recognized the sex. The perfume was new. "We're not playing a game, Charlie."

"You making something out of two people standing in a room?"

I closed the door and walked to the center of the room.

She stood in front of the table and chair smiling. "You look good. You're not the skinny kid I remember."

"You forced me to kill a man."

She sighed like a little girl who didn't get the Christmas gift she wanted. "I didn't make you do anything, Johnny. I wasn't there that night. The police found me at home baking bread for my man. I even wore an apron. Can you imagine?"

"You knew about the coke, but instead of telling me so we could run away, you took some and sent me back to Egorov short. You sent me knowing he would kill me."

"I took risks, too! If you hadn't killed him, he would have come after me. But I believed in you. I knew you had it in you." She shrugged. "The trial just didn't go the way we wanted."

"What did you think would happen? The cops would let me off and we'd take over Egorov's drug business? The Russians replaced him within a week while I sat in prison for twelve years."

"It made you a better man, Johnny."

"A better man? I spent every day and night thinking about all the ways I wanted to kill you. I loved you hard right up until the day they closed the door on my prison cell. You destroyed me, Charlie."

"Johnny, you're a sweet boy, you're a good boy. Don't go mucking around in areas you know nothing about."

"Imagining you dead kept me warm at night."

She licked her lips, smiled. "You say the sexiest things to a girl." She laughed. "I like being in your dreams all those years. I've never received so much attention from a man, though many have tried. I thought about you occasionally, especially late at night. I wondered how prison would treat you. You were always weak, Johnny. Even now, you're obsessed with the past. You need to move on."

I remained silent.

She brought the gun up, stared at it: a Glock 17. Too large for her hands, too large for her intentions. The tendons in her hand flexed as her finger played with the trigger.

"It's not a toy."

She shrugged. "I've shot guns before."

She let the gun drop to her side, the barrel pointed at the floor. She wiggled forward, her body moving with a seductive rhythm. Quiet purring sounds emanated from the depths of the oversized coat, but I felt no arousal, just a cold ache in my chest and a morning breath taste in my mouth.

I pushed her into the chair. She landed with an unfeminine grunt. Her coat spilled open, and she spread across the chair like a bottle of creamy white milk. She pointed the gun at my chest. A snarl erupted from her. "Touch me like that again, *please*."

I leaned in, my hands on the arms of the chair, the gun barrel touching my chest. "Pull the god damn trigger, Charlie."

The snarl faded, her lips parted in a kiss. "You've changed, Johnny. Oh, boy have you changed."

She set the gun on the table. I stepped back as she leaned forward, her watery brown eyes searching mine. "Foreplay makes me hungry. Do you want the full meal?"

My hands shook. I badly wanted to slap the hell out of her. She purred, sensing my desire to hurt her. She would let me do it and would laugh afterwards with those big nasty eyes while she licked the blood off my knuckles.

"Do you have something you want to do?" she asked. "Do you want to teach me about prison life?"

"You need to leave."

"Oh, Johnny, why don't you want to play? You've become so good at it." She crossed her legs, flipped the coat closed, but it was too short to cover a strip of leg above her boots. "At least prison didn't change everything about you."

"One day you will find out how much I've changed."

"You need to take your promises seriously, Johnny. I've been disappointed too many times by men who couldn't keep their word."

I sat down on the bed. "Why are you here?"

"You need to stay out of Tancredi's business."

"Did he send you?"

"No."

"Why are you here?"

"You and I were friends once. I'm offering you some friendly advice."

"What do you know about him?"

"He likes to hurt people and their families."

"He a friend of yours?"

"Professional associate."

"Should I care?"

"You know, when I heard you got out of prison and tangled up with his men I imagined for a minute you did it for me."

"How are you involved with Tancredi?"

"Nobody is. That man keeps everyone at leash length. I thought—I thought maybe you came back for me. I thought we could repair what we had."

"You can't repair that."

"Let me try to make amends, please? I can get you information on Tancredi. That's got to matter to you."

"You told me to leave him alone. Now you want to rat on him. Charlie, you're all over the map. What the hell's the matter with you?"

"He's a bastard, Johnny. He hurts people."

"Are you sleeping with him?"

She bit her lip. "He keeps a stable of us. I haven't seen him in three months, which means my turn's coming up."

"He pay your bills?"

"Most of them." She frowned. "Roy told me you were back in town. The poor fool, he tried hurting me with the information. He expected a reaction, only I didn't have one. I'm dead inside, Johnny, been that way a long time. Tancredi beat out everything that mattered. I'm used to it now but sometimes it still hurts. Sometimes I still want to live."

I shrugged. "I'm tired, Charlie. Go home. You've got nothing I want."

"Maybe I have what Tancredi wants?"

I pulled her to her feet, twisted her arm around until she

cried out. I picked up the gun and pressed it against her knee. "You can't work the streets if you can't walk."

A naked snarling animal in a high dollar coat, she stared at me with hatred. "You son of a bitch, I'm not a whore."

I tossed the gun onto the bed and slapped her hard across her cheek.

She laughed. "You learned a few things in prison! You never used to hate women."

"I don't hate women, Charlie, I hate *you*. I hate you because of what you did. You're a nasty little creature."

She would never see the monster she had become, but I could see in her eyes she glimpsed it.

"I'll be glad when he kills you," she said.

"I believe you."

"You got the gun. You could kill me now. Do it!"

"Be a good little tramp and get on the next barge out of town, Charlie. I've got too many other things to do."

Her eyes widened, her mind calculating all the different ways she could use me. She gave me a look I couldn't describe before, but understood now. I was a tool, like a gun or a hammer, to be exploited and manipulated for her own ends. She would try to stay ahead of me, figure out which direction I would go so she could put things in front of me she wanted destroyed. She shook her head. "Nobody can win against these guys, not even you. There's no point in doing this."

"I can and I will."

She slid on to the floor looking up at me, her breasts naked, her neck tilted towards me, the slap on her cheek growing darker. "Johnny, let's work it out, please? You can do whatever you want with me. I'm yours."

I stepped back, picked up the gun, tossed it to her. "Get out of here."

Tears rolled down her cheeks as she stared at the still too large gun. "I loved you. I loved you more than anything in the world. Why did you come back? You can't get justice. There's no such thing. You going to play the knight, make everybody safe? You can't do it. There's no safety in this world. You can't do it. You can't go from being what you were to what you want to be. You were nothing then and you're nothing now."

"Who are you talking about?"

She stood up, put the gun in her pocket. "You're bigger, meaner, but you're the same failure you were when we were kids. I had to push you. I always had to push you. You're a typical guy: lazy with no ambition. Men kill to sleep with me, you stupid son of a bitch, but I gave myself to you and what do you do with it? Nothing. You wanted to be boring. You wanted a girlfriend and I wanted to be a queen. I would have made you a king!" The tears came harder now, causing her body to shake. "Why the hell won't you take me, use me like all the other men do?"

"You're broken and twisted, rotted all the way through."

"You're a son of a bitch."

"You're repeating yourself, Charlie."

The tears disappeared with a single swipe of her sleeve. Her breathing relaxed and only the soft glisten of her eyes remained. A smile graced her lips, the smile she'd perfected many years ago as her final method of disarming me.

She lingered, as if relishing the moment before she spoke. Her voice steady, she said, "You didn't ask about your son."

My first week in prison she visited and told me she was pregnant. She stood up and walked out. I spent months writing, calling, trying desperately to get her attention. Was it a boy—a girl? I didn't care which. I had a child.

I found out later she aborted it.

She searched for a reaction, some admission of pain. It was the only thing she could see, emotion, and the worse the better. It was why we'd found each other. I was a train wreck and she was a lover of train wrecks. I smashed everything and she loved seeing things smashed. She couldn't stop but could I?

"Johnny—" She took a deep breath, let it out slowly. Sweat glistened on her forehead. "Johnny, I'm sorry I hurt you."

I said nothing.

"I know I hurt you. I can't make it up to you. I can't make it like it was. But you have to know, I never loved Tancredi. Not like you. I never even married him. But he cares about me, though, you know? Why can't you walk away from him? He's done nothing to you, not really. Nothing that can't be fixed by money. He's got a lot. He can give you some. You can leave town and never come back."

"You never quit."

"You're making me choose."

"You picked your side when you didn't tell me about the drugs."

"I'm scared. Help me, please?"

"You deserve Tancredi."

"I'm sorry! If I could go back and change everything, I would."

I shook my head. "You should have left town when I went to prison. You should have left before you got involved with Tancredi. You should leave now."

"There has to be a chance for us!"

"We're toxic. You destroy things."

A motel notepad sat on the table next to her. She wrote her number on it with a shaking hand. "Call me, Johnny. You'll call me." She pressed two wet lips onto the bottom of the page. Tears stained the page. "You'll call me. Yes, you will." She stood up. She wasn't talking to me any longer. "You'll call me because you'll want to know what I know. I'll tell you everything. You know why?"

I said nothing.

"I'll tell you because I love you and you love me. We're meant to be together."

She closed her coat, pressed her hands into the pockets. Tears ran down her cheeks. "I couldn't have shot you, not you, Johnny. Anybody else I could...maybe. But I guess we're like that you and me. We want to pull the trigger and hurt one another. Maybe it's just a way to hurt ourselves. I don't know...Look at me, all messed up. I guess it's always that way with you."

I opened the door. "Get out of town, Charlie. It's the only chance you got."

FOURTEEN

I arrived at Kelly's shop at nine the next morning. The unlit sign had collected more snow in the evening so now all but the Υ was covered. I made the first tracks of the day up to the side door, found it locked and hunted around for the spare key Julian had shown me.

Inside I turned on all the lights and heaters and found the manifest for the first job of the day, then I dug in and started working. I replaced a radiator and two full sets of brakes by the afternoon and still neither Julian or Kelly had called in or shown up. I went into Kelly's office and dug around until I found employee files, flipped through the folders until I found an entry for Julian which contained an address but no telephone number. I called a taxi and gave the driver the address.

Julian's house sat on a corner in a quiet neighborhood. Snow plows had cleared the streets and homeowners had cleared the sidewalks. Children lay in one yard swishing their arms and legs back and forth making snow angels near a partially constructed snowman. They didn't notice as I exited the cab and walked up to Julian's front door.

I rang the buzzer. My breath puffed out in front of me while I watched the windows for movement. Finally, a shape came forward, fiddled at the lock and opened the door.

The woman frowning at me stood about five feet tall, wore her light brown hair in a wavy cascade around her wide curvy face and had two big dimples buttoning her together. Big watery eyes focused sharply upon me, curious and hostile. "Yes?"

"Ashley?"

"No, I'm her sister."

"Is she around? Is Julian around?"

"No. They're at the hospital."

"The hospital?"

"They've been there since last night."

"What happened?"

"Julian got hurt is all I know."

I looked up the street. No way I would get a taxi from here within an hour. "Do you have a car?"

"I'm not giving you a ride. I have to go to work in an hour."

"Which hospital is it?"

"University. It's not on my way to work and you can't walk there in this weather. You'll freeze."

"What's the address?"

She told me and she pointed in the general direction.

"Do you have a phone? I need to call a taxi."

"Who are you?"

"I work with Julian at the auto repair shop."

She stared at me skeptically. "Wait out here, I'll call."

I protested but she closed the door. I stood outside, my hands buried in my coat, watching the children work on their snowman. They had most of the body completed when

Ashley's sister returned to the door and said, "They'll be here in twenty minutes."

"May I stand in the doorway?" I asked.

She did all those calculations a person does to decide whether they should trust a stranger enough to let them stand in their home for an indeterminate amount of time.

I smiled at her.

She let me inside. "Fine. But no small talk. I hate small talk."

Under her attentive suspicious gaze, I did exactly what I said I would do. I stood quietly on the small square of linoleum just inside the front door making a sad puddle with the snow from my boots, while I pretended to watch the obnoxiously loud television.

When the taxi came, I said thank you and climbed in as fast as I could. I looked back and saw her peeking through the living room curtains, the television flickering behind her.

The cab driver drove me through the maze of the city and dropped me off at the front entrance of the hospital. I saw nothing until I stepped into room 214 and found Julian asleep under a thick layer of hospital blankets. His left arm protruded at a sharp angle, held up with a cast. Fresh bandages wrapped his head in a puffy shell.

An older pregnant version of the woman I had just spent twenty minutes with looked up as I walked into the room.

"Who are you?" she asked.

"I work with Julian."

She frowned. "He had dinner with you last night."

I nodded. "We had burgers and he dropped me off at my place, said he was going home."

She glanced at Julian. "He didn't come home. The police called me after eight, said they found him in an alley. They think he was robbed but they don't know. The doctors

93

operated on him this morning. They don't know if he will wake up."

"I'm sorry."

"You're sorry? Why are you sorry?"

"What do you think happened?"

She laughed. "He wasn't robbed that's for sure. He wouldn't let any single guy beat him up, not like that. It had to be two, maybe three of them. And they jumped him from behind. The doctors mentioned the crack on his skull came from behind."

"Where did this happen?"

"In the alley behind The Broken Dove. He doesn't drink there. I don't know why he was there."

Julian lay in the bed wrapped in a mess of clean white bandages. Wires held his purpled jaw in place and long strips of gauze covered one eye. The other eye opened, glanced around wildly, caught sight of me. His whole body shook. From the depth of his throat he groaned something like my name.

I leaned in. "Yeah?"

"Lester…Black…Hair…Dirk…"

"*Blond*," I said. "The two goons from the other night. Got it. Stop talking." I touched his shoulder, but it was covered in so many bandages I couldn't tell if he felt it. "Close your eye. Get some sleep."

He closed his eye. His body sagged. I stepped back, pulled the wad of money from my pocket and peeled off a few bills. I put these in my pocket and left the rest on the bedside tray. "Vandals smashed up Kelly's shop. Julian tried to find out who did it," I said to no one in particular.

"Do you feel guilty?" Ashley asked, looking at the money.

"He did what he thought was right. I'm doing the same."

"We were supposed to be married at the beginning of the

year. Now we'll be lucky if he's awake. Why did he do it? Why did he risk everything? He's already so banged up inside."

"He thought these men needed to be stopped and thought he could help. It was important to him."

"He's not important, not to them. He's important to me. I need him. I need him safe. He should never have helped you."

"He didn't help me. He helped himself. Without the shop, he has no job, which means no work and no money when the baby arrives."

I left her touching her belly and frowning.

FIFTEEN

I paid the cab driver from my few remaining bills and walked into the Broken Dove with almost empty pockets. The bar was loud, jovial and dark. On a foot high stage in the far corner three young men sweated out steel guitar covers through battered amplifiers. The crowd didn't care that the band played out of tune and a little out of sync; the music was loud and familiar and their beer glasses never stayed empty. They looked comfortable and relaxed; locals hanging out at their neighborhood bar on a Thursday night.

I found a seat at the bar next to a couple sitting quietly watching the band, ordered a beer and scanned the crowd for the two men from Kelly's shop. Neither man made an appearance. The band played another song; the couple ordered more drinks while I nursed mine. Music erupted from the speakers too loud to ask the bartender about the men and no one else appeared the type to ask. I saw khakis and office scan badges and wedding bands, not items I associated with the two junkies from Kelly's shop.

The distribution of women to men appeared roughly

three to one. Maybe it was ladies' night, maybe it wasn't; I enjoyed the view either way. Tall, short, blonde or brunette; some showed off skin, others not enough. I watched each as they passed by, never ogling, never rude, but always with a convict's eye. Some stopped by the bar to get a drink and I made eye contact with a nod. They smelled of lavender, vanilla, sweat and drunkenness, all the scents of hungry women. Some returned the nod or even tried a conversation, but eventually they moved on and I didn't mind. I wasn't here to talk, and the band did a good job preventing it.

The band changed twice while I nursed warm beers. In between sets I asked the bartender for the time and she said ten thirty. I considered leaving, but she said the band stopped at eleven. I said thanks and ordered another beer intending to stay until the end.

The couple next to me left, and the space filled with a half dozen college age kids smiling and apologizing, but determined to wiggle their way in to the space made for two. They blocked my view of the door so I picked up my drink and walked around to the other side of the bar. I did the same squeezing act as the college kids to a group of women who smiled politely but quickly dismissed me. The doorman stood about three feet wide by six feet tall, which was enough to block most of the entrance, but he stood to one side and I could see down the length of the hall well enough to notice anyone before they got to him. I settled in at my new perch and watched the crowd.

This late in the evening, the workers required to have a drink with the boss or celebrate an awkward office birthday had left. The crowd had turned younger and more eager to drink. I watched them ebb and flow around the room, maintaining my view of the door. Occasionally the door opened letting in drafts of cold air. I appreciated it after the cloying scents of spilled beer and sweating bodies at the back of the bar. The group of women next to me continued their steady march towards drunkenness with loud calls for more rounds of green drinks, so I missed the entrance of one of the men who had done a number on me.

Lester has black hair, Julian had said, which meant Dirk had blond.

Black hair. Lester. He sat at a front row table so close to an amplifier I wondered if he was deaf. Two drinks, both empty, sat on a tiny table in front of him. Bandages covered the left side of his head and a sling held his left arm tight against his body. The damage made me grin and then frown. I couldn't imagine Lester jumping Julian, not with that sling. Maybe Julian had done the work himself. Good for him. No matter what horror story Lester had crawled back and spun for his boss, he had no imagination to describe what was about to happen to him.

I started towards the table when the waitress dropped off two more beers. *Two beers.* An empty chair sat next to Lester, the beer in front of it. I glanced around, but saw no one in the crowd who looked like Dirk. The restrooms lined the back wall. I pushed my way through the crowd and entered the men's room. One toilet stall and two urinals filled the small room which stank of beer, vomit and lemon.

Dirk stood at the right urinal with his back to me. I locked the door behind me and then ran at him, head down, shoulder leveled at his neck. My shoulder connected against his spine just between his shoulder blades. His head snapped back and jerked forward when his body hit the urinal. His face smacked against the concrete wall and sprayed blood over the chrome piping. Overhead the dangling light jiggled casting wild shadows about the room. Holding my right fist with my left hand I brought my right elbow down on his collar. There was a pop and he dropped to his knees. I grabbed his head in both hands and slammed his teeth down on the bottom edge of the urinal. Blood and teeth swirled around a pink wafer as he fell backwards onto the floor, glazed eyes staring up at me, bubbles of bloody foam building at the sides of his mouth.

I stepped back, breathing hard. He would live.

I unlocked the door and left the room. The band announced their final song and kicked into it as the crowd roared their approval. I pushed through them, receiving several shocked glances. I wiped my face and found blood on my hand.

Lester sat at the table with a beer in his one good hand. Blue, red, and green lights flashed overhead, reflecting off the band's silver guitars. I stepped past someone blocking his view. Apparently, I took too long because he yelled at me to move the hell out of the way. The noise caught Lester's attention. He turned and saw me. I was a big dark shape flashing under stage lights. He stood up just as I came upon him.

Lester stood chest high, drunk, already yelling at me or around me—maybe for Dirk—but I couldn't hear him. I brought my knee up into his groin. His eyes widened. He fumbled forward unbalanced with only one good arm. Planting my feet, I swung my right fist into the side of his head. The blow caught his ear, tore into the cartilage and soft part of his ear canal. He stumbled sideways into a chair which he tried to use to right himself. His arm got entangled between the seat and the back. I brought my foot down on his shoulder. Ligaments tore free of bone, muscles twitched uselessly and the joint separated. His body convulsed. His face, a mix of blood and snot and tears, turned towards me in a silent scream.

A woman behind us screamed for him.

The band had stopped playing. The singer held his microphone inches from his mouth in a silent pose. The lights went out. Feedback screeched through the amplifiers. Tables scraped the floor, glass broke, the lights popped back on and the room came alive in an ugly nasty mess. People trampled one another rushing towards the door. Some tripped over chairs or tables or slipped on spilled drinks. A sign over the main door said EXIT in bright red letters. Less than five feet away, next to the main stage, was a fire door.

I stepped through it into the cold evening air of the alley. People raced past the mouth of the alley. Police sirens wailed in the distance. I turned the other direction and disappeared around the corner.

SIXTEEN

Munroe was yelling as he crashed through the door of Kelly's shop, "What the hell were you thinking?"

I stood in the bay with a carburetor mounted in a vice. I had spent most of the morning cleaning it and reworking the gaskets. Occasionally the cleaning solvent would sting my scraped knuckles.

"You needed to maintain a low profile! What the hell was that?"

"What was *what?*"

"Last night, you son of a bitch. I told you to behave yourself. You put those men in the hospital for a month."

Setting my cleaning rag down, I faced him. "You've known about Lou's trouble for a long time, you just didn't do anything about it. Maybe you thought you couldn't do anything. Maybe you were just weak."

"Go to hell."

"But you're a smart bastard. You put me right in the middle of it, knowing I'd do something. You didn't care what so long as it caused problems for everybody but Lou."

"You need to watch what you say."

I walked towards him. He wore a different suit; this one had more wrinkles. "Stop playing games with me, Munroe. You're trying to be a good cop, don't muddy it up by lying to me."

"I didn't know those men."

"No, but you knew who they worked for. You knew men like that would come. Lou's been getting pressure from all sides. You wanted to help but didn't know how."

"You put those men in the hospital for months."

"You said that."

"Do you think your response was justified?"

"Those *criminals* got what they deserved."

"You're not a judge."

"And you are? I remember what you said at the prison."

"I'm a cop. My job is to arrest people, to turn them over to the courts to be judged by the system."

I grinned at him. "Your system is broken. Has been for a long time, but nobody is willing to do anything about it."

"They're going to come for you."

I stood in Munroe's face. Out of prison, standing before him with no handcuffs, no guards, I was taller and bigger and faster. "Who's coming for me, *Detective*?"

"Do you want to go up against me, Brogan? I'll take you down right here. I'll put your ass in that trash can and take you to the landfill myself."

"You won't," I said. "You smoke two packs a day and sit behind a desk the rest of the time. Any exercise you get is company mandated. You're nothing but an over the hill ball player who's good at intimidating junkies. It won't work on me."

He licked his lips. Wiped his mouth. "Tancredi," he said, looking away.

I stepped back and shrugged. "I'm going to continue working today. If somebody comes for me, they come for me. If I have to put them in the hospital, I will."

"You think it's that simple? They beat you up, you beat them up more? Do you think you're in a schoolyard fight over milk money? It's about to escalate."

"Yes, but not for those two. They served their purpose. The next men to come will doubt themselves. At the wrong time, they'll think of the men in the hospital and they'll realize they don't want to suck their food through a straw. Maybe they tell themselves it can't happen to them, but it can and they know it so it'll cost them their edge."

"Tancredi's not like that."

"I'm not talking about Tancredi. I'm talking about the flunkies. I'm talking about the low-level guys who don't stand a chance. They'll think twice which means most won't even show up."

"I didn't get you out so you could make a mess."

"Want me to ask them politely to leave Lou alone? I'd be willing to try if you think it would work."

"We interviewed people at the bar. You didn't even give them a chance."

"A chance to do what? Hurt me? Munroe, you're a cop. You've seen the worst people can do. You're right I didn't give them a chance. This is a war I didn't start but I'm going to finish it. I fight to win and last night was just the start."

"Tancredi won't throw tweakers at you next time. He's going to send men with guns, a lot of guns."

"Line them up. I'll knock them down one per coffin."

His face twitched, his lips torn back in a sneer. "You don't care if you die."

I shook my head. "You don't get it. I know who the enemy is now, and I know the choices they've made to become my enemy. Those choices have consequences. They could have chosen a different path, but they chose violence and violence is what I'll give them."

"You're scared of Egorov. You're hoping you'll get killed."

"You're wrong, Munroe. I very much like breathing. I'll do it long after Tancredi and much longer than Egorov."

He pulled a cigarette from his coat. His yellowed fingers shook in the cold. "Why can't you turn on some heat around here?"

I laughed.

"Not that kind of heat. It's freezing in here."

"The heater is on in Lou's office."

He looked at the office, shook his head.

I shrugged.

"Where is he?"

"I haven't seen him for a couple of days."

Munroe inhaled smoke from his cigarette, exhaled through his nose and coughed. He inadvertently tossed the lit butt into a can of used engine oil and frowned. He looked at me.

"Has anyone around here taken a science class?" I asked.

"Why didn't it light?"

"Go back to high school."

He turned away from the butt floating in the oil and said, "We can move you."

"I'm right where I want to be. Everyone says the city is broken and they can't do anything about it. It's a lie they tell themselves so they can sleep at night. I don't lie. Not to them and not to myself. I don't want violence, but I will use it to defend what's important."

"God damn it, Brogan. You're talking like a machine. Like you felt nothing. Don't you feel regret? Guilt maybe?"

"Our paths wouldn't have crossed if those two hadn't taken money to smash up Lou's shop."

Munroe shook his head. "You and Lou. I should never have put you two together."

I waited for him to get to the point.

"These things," he said, indicating the car. "These things are magic. You turn the little silver key and they go, just like that. All that oil and noise and plastic and metal, it don't mean shit. Could be squirrels or leprechauns for all it matters once the hood is closed. But a car is like a girlfriend in the sense that you get used to her usual noises. Only, when she squeaks wrong or chugs along all spotty and doesn't have the same giddy up as she used to, you take notice. Because just like a woman, if she ain't purring all pretty like, it will cost you a stack of pennies."

"Get to the point."

"I don't understand cars or women. I sleep next to my wife damn near every night, but I really don't know what's going on in her head. She worries about drapes and matching plates and all kinds of things I don't understand or care about. But you get me near a drug dealer or convict and that I understand. He does all kinds of stupid things I understand like I can read his mind. But you, you I don't understand. There's something wrong with you. There's something in you I don't understand. And I don't like that. It's not normal or right."

"What are you talking about?"

"The woman with a gun."

"Who?"

"Do a lot of women point guns at you?"

"What about her?"

"Who was she?"

"Nobody."

"Nobody? A complete stranger comes into your room, points a gun at you and she's nobody?"

"You wired the room."

"We wired the room."

I smiled at him, big and wide and toothy. "Then I don't need to tell you anything."

"You knew we wired the room. That's why you tried to provoke her, to see if we'd give away our position. You son of a bitch, you're tainting this case."

"I didn't know you wired the room, but, whether I did or not, you don't need to worry about her. She's the past."

"She wanted you to slap her around, beat her up. She practically begged you to kill her. That's what's called a rogue element. Rogue elements get cases thrown out. I can't have my witness discrediting himself because of an insane girlfriend. Do you understand me? All this work gets dumped in the river. You understand?"

"You said nothing about testifying."

He lit another cigarette. "What the hell did you think this was about? It's about putting Egorov behind bars. It's about shutting down the corruption in this city."

"You put me on the stand and every thug in this city will try cutting me down."

Munroe shook his head. "You stupid son of a bitch. What do you think you've been doing? You're standing up begging for somebody to come knock you down. And they're going to."

I said nothing.

"I'm not as behind as you think I am," he said. "That woman was your ex, Charlie. I listened to those tapes a half dozen times and I realized something. You tripped up on something you said."

I waited.

"You told me you didn't know about the drugs, but you told Charlie something different."

"Charlie knew about the drugs, I didn't."

"You knew she took them."

"I knew afterwards. I figured it out during my trial. Sometimes I brought the packages home because a shop closed for the day or I got a bad address or bad directions. I'd try the delivery the next morning, going back to Egorov only if I absolutely had to."

"You did it often enough and Charlie got curious one time."

I nodded. "She must have cut one of them open and found the drugs. I remember she became curious about my work for a while but I thought nothing of it. I thought she was interested in me."

"She planned to steal the drugs."

"Yes."

"Your girlfriend knows you're carrying dope and, instead of getting you out of the mess, she puts you deeper into it." Munroe whistled. "Twelve years, that's got to bother you. I'm surprised she's still walking the streets after what she did to you."

"You heard the tape."

"Ugly world we live in."

"What's the latest on Petr? Is he here yet?"

Another cigarette. This time he coughed twice trying to get it lit. He looked at me daring me to say something. "We haven't heard anything."

"Do you have anybody looking? From what I understand, the people who work for him here don't know what he looks like. He's just a name."

"He's *not* just a name. He's had over a dozen men killed in the last two years. But you're right, only the Russians see him. Nobody knows anything about him beyond that. But yes, we're looking for him."

"Shouldn't this be a Federal case?"

Munroe shook his head. "As far as they're concerned he's done his time. And besides, they don't expect him to show up."

"You do?"

"Would you go after the guy who killed your brother?"

"Depends on my brother."

"We can put you back in prison if we want."

"We?"

"My boss had me up at five this morning listening to your tapes. She wants you on a shorter leash." Munroe shook his head. "I don't know when the woman sleeps."

"I saw Charlie two nights ago. You took this long to listen to the tapes?"

Munroe coughed.

I grabbed his coat. Greased smeared his shirt. "There is no team, is there? It's just the two of you. Are you running an illegal operation to get Petr Egorov?"

Munroe brought his hands up between mine, brought his elbows down on my collar bones. A smooth motion, much faster than I expected. I stumbled backwards, gagging on the stench of his breath and the pain in my shoulders.

"Never put your hands on me," he said calmly. "I don't give a damn how pissed off you are."

I leaned against the workbench coughing and rubbing my collar bones.

"Where's the gun?" Munroe asked.

"What gun?"

"The gun Charlie left behind in your motel room."

"She took it with her."

He leaned in. "I listened to the tape. She didn't take the gun with her. I never heard her pick it up."

"Go to hell, Munroe. I don't have it."

"You poor bastard. This woman's just got you all kinds of messed up. First, she gets you put away for twelve years, then she walks back into your life ready to shoot you. What the hell is it with you two?"

"It's complicated."

"Fine. Get your coat. You can tell it to my boss."

SEVENTEEN

Munroe made small talk on the drive, but when I only grunted in response, he gave up and lit a cigarette.

We parked in front of a generic two story office building. Silver plaques next to each office door advertised their purpose: dentistry, insurance and real estate made up most of the tenants. I followed Munroe up the stairs to the second floor and down a dark hallway to an office with no silver plaque and a wood door instead of glass. He fumbled with a ring of keys in the lock, tried one and then another.

"Is it unlocked?" I asked.

He tried the door. It opened. He scowled at me saying nothing.

A row of desks sat on either side of a long aisle. The desks contained lamps and power cords for non-existent electronics. At the end of the aisle a large window looked into an office with a single desk. Munroe led me to the office.

Inside, sitting behind a desk, we found a woman. Her eyes watched us walk into the room where they pinned us to the carpet. Over a pair of thin glasses resting on the bridge of her nose, the eyes were an unnatural blue contrasted by sharp eyebrows, long, thick, raven hair, and dark Latin skin. She wore a blue suit over a silver blouse and a thin silver necklace. She was in her mid-thirties. Typed pages with hand-written notes and manila folders lay before her. "You're late."

I grinned at her. "You must be the boss."

Munroe frowned, she remained expressionless. Not glancing at the paperwork, she turned it over and standing, held out her hand. "Eryn Harker."

I shook her hand and, unlike her eyes, it was warm. "Why am I here?"

Munroe pulled up a chair and sat. "You're here because you were told to be here."

I looked around for a chair. Two of them lined the wall; both covered with stacks of paper. I remained standing. "This case can't be producing this much paperwork."

Harker sat, took the glasses off, folded them and placed them in a felt lined case. "You're here because I wanted to meet you."

"Anything else?"

She smiled. "Gun toting ex-girlfriends and tweakers with wired jaws don't interest me."

"Do you expect a justification?"

"No. I'm interested in you, Brogan. I wondered if you could handle what was coming. Let's call next week the big game and let's chock the last five days up as training accidents."

"I'm not playing a game."

"Neither am I. I must justify you being loose to my bosses. Your behavior is making that difficult."

"Your bosses? Is this operation sanctioned?"

"It is. In a way. It's under another case with a different

aim."

"Which is why there's only two of you."

Munroe chuckled.

I shook my head. "You dangled me out as bait but you caught a different fish. It's Egorov you want, but Munroe has me angled towards Tancredi. Why?"

Harker sat back in her chair, crossed her legs under the desk. She brought her arms up and crossed them over her breasts. Munroe coughed but I didn't look at him.

"Detective Munroe put you there to keep tabs on you. It's unfortunate you stirred up Tancredi but it helps. We had him under a three-year investigation which stalled six months ago when we pulled our agent from the river."

"Did they know he was a cop?"

"He had 'cop' cut into his forehead, chest, legs and arms so that we would get the message no matter what the fish did to him."

"He killed one of your own, why haven't you gone after him harder?"

"We tried. When the criminals wear organizational colors or particular styles of clothes, inserting undercover agents is much easier. But when they do this," she flipped open a folder and tossed it onto the desk, "we can't get near them. Initiation involves mutilation and scarring the likes of which we can't do. It doesn't matter if it's Russians, Chinese, Columbians or even locals, the requirement is you scar yourself to show how little you matter compared to the group. It's a loyalty test."

I glanced through the photos: genital mutilation, missing digits and facial tattoos dominated.

Munroe snorted. "God damn savages. And now Tancredi is involved with them."

"You need to stay focused," Harker said. "Tancredi and

his gang are not your target. You need to stay away from them."

"Munroe thinks otherwise."

"Stay focused, Brogan. I can't have you getting shot."

"Live bait attracts bigger fish. I made sure Tancredi would come for me. I can't stop him now."

"And if you could?"

"He's done enough to piss me off."

"Leave him alone."

I shook my head. "Tancredi won't retreat and neither will I."

"Two bulls in a ring? Machismo in this day and age?"

"If I thought asking him to be a good human being would change his ways, I would ask him. But he won't. He hurts people so he needs to be stopped."

"He'll kill you. He's not a tweaker thug or diner rapist. Yes, I know about that. Did you consider the danger you're putting your waitress in?"

"You keep her out of this."

"I can't make promises."

"You bring her in, you can forget my help."

"We can protect her."

"No you can't. The gloves are off now. The stakes increased. Munroe said it himself. I'm telling, so we're clear, any one comes at me, I kill them. I don't care who it is."

Harker turned to Munroe. "You were smart to bring him in."

"He doesn't learn. I blame the limited penitentiary educational system."

"You're wrong," I said. "You're wasting time writing up reports nobody reads because you're hiding. You know it's not the way to catch these guys but you're afraid to act. They're animals. You kill them."

"I will not debate you."

"You don't have to. I didn't come here for your opinion. I came here to find out your plan to stop me."

"We can put you back in prison."

"A waste of time. You want Tancredi dead and you want Egorov dead. I don't understand why you won't admit it to yourself."

Munroe coughed. Harker stared at him. She turned to me. "We're not the executioners. We're the cops. We arrest criminals."

"You're beyond that. Nobody is doing the job anymore. You arrest Tancredi or anyone else they'll be back on the street in the morning and you'll have a target on your back."

"Where is the gun the ex gave you?"

I shook my head. "She took it when she left."

"At least you're not killing civilians yet."

I took a deep breath and let the comment go.

She frowned. "I'm sorry. You want a gun, get it off the street. We're not arms dealers."

Munroe reached for a cigarette, but stopped at a glance from Harker.

Harker flipped through another folder tossing it open on the table. "We have the time and the length of the calls but nothing else. Tancredi is using encryption we can't break. We think he's cutting a deal, but we don't know what he's getting."

"What about Egorov?"

"Nothing."

"Nothing?"

"There's no chatter anywhere on him."

"How are you getting transcripts if they're using encryption?"

"Tancredi is using the encryption. We think upgrading the

Russian tech is part of what he's offering them."

"And they've said nothing about Petr?"

"Not that we've seen."

I turned to Munroe. "Drop me off at Kelly's."

Munroe glanced at Harker. She nodded.

"Sure," he said.

EIGHTEEN

Munroe stopped the car in Kelly's lot and shoved the transmission into park. He stared ahead, but when I grabbed the door handle, he said, "I want to live in a clean city, too, but there's a process. You can't kill the criminals and not call yourself a tyrant."

"Whatever helps you sleep at night."

I stepped out of the car and let in the cold. "I'm done with the motel so you can clear out your bugs. I'll find you when I'm ready."

"We're on the same—"

I closed the door and trudged through the snow to the shop. Munroe spun the car around and raced out of the parking lot. I waited until his tail lights disappeared around a corner and went into the shop.

My breath hung in the air as I stood in the bay listening. A clock ticked away the time over Kelly's office. An air compressor made a single hissing pop as it performed its pressure check. I stomped my boots to kick off the gray slush then went into Kelly's office. I turned on the space heater next to the desk. The air filled with the smell of hot metal.

Back in the bay I put my overalls on and reviewed the work manifest. Several notes in Julian's scratchy handwriting indicated that the Ford sitting on the stand required a muffler and spark plugs. The parts I found stacked neatly on a shelf in one corner with the manifest details taped to them. Kelly ran a tight shop and I liked that. I laid out the tools, raised the truck on its platform and started working.

I thought about Munroe: an honest cop in a corrupt city. I wondered what he expected to gain. Removing men like Tancredi had little effect on the city. Dozens of men were ready to fill the vacuum, the same as when I killed Boris.

I wondered what kind of leverage Munroe's bosses had on him. Detectives have lieutenants and captains and all kinds of elected representatives above them shouting out their rules and their orders.

The honest bosses apply the kind of pressure a detective needs—follow the procedures, catch the bad guys—it's the bad bosses that do the real damage. They redirect the detective off the criminals that matter and onto the smalltime busts that look good in the paper, but have no real effect on the street. The problem is compounded when more than one boss is dirty.

Letting me out of prison spoke of corruption from top to bottom. Egorov's cronies could have used an honest DA, an honest judge and manipulated the process. Maybe Munroe was one of the honest ones—at least as honest as one could be in a situation like this. He knew the corruption existed, he knew how it worked and he moved within it. Did that make him bad? What mental twists and turns does an existence like that require of a good cop?

I tumbled through these questions and more throughout the morning and into the afternoon, until the side door popped open and a man in his forties with slick black hair and a dark tan entered. He wore a cashmere suit and a heavy overcoat. Behind him two guys wearing black suits and damp raincoats squeezed through the door.

I was impressed. I had given Tancredi twenty hour hours to make his way back to Kelly's and he'd done it in eighteen. That made him smarter than I expected.

"Hello?" A pause and then, "Where the hell is everybody? I thought you said somebody was in here."

I climbed out of the pit with my hands empty and greasy.

"Who are you?" Tancredi asked.

The henchmen fanned out appraising me in a relaxed manner. In my blue overalls and greasy hands, they saw me as an honest sucker scraping to earn a living. They turned away searching for the threat.

"Don't look at them," Tancredi said. "Look at me. Who are you?"

"Brogan," I said.

"Brogan. I don't know that name. You somebody I should know?"

"You know me, I'm the guy who busted up your junkies the other night."

Tancredi smiled. "Maybe I have heard of you. You got a knack for sticking your nose where it don't belong."

The henchmen faced me with renewed interest. Both stood up taller, leaned forward into their stances. One loosened his coat.

"Where's your boss?"

"He didn't come in today," I said. "The weather's got him down."

"Too bad. I wanted to file a customer service complaint against you."

"Understandable. I've never been too good with dogs

when they make messes."

"You're funny."

"Your boys, I hear, will be eating baby food through straws for a long time. If these two keep dancing around like they are, same thing will happen to them."

The henchmen froze. They'd moved forward while we talked. They watched me, waiting for the word from Tancredi.

Tancredi laughed. "Our little fly has a bite. Did your boss teach you that? Would be a shame if something happened to him."

"It would," I said. "Anything happens to him but old age, you'll be the first person I visit." I scratched at my chin. "I may visit you, anyway. I could offer tips on remodeling. After seeing the work done on this place I got a few new ideas."

"Are you threatening me, Brogan?"

"I thought we were talking about interior design. Do you want to change the subject?"

He showed teeth, straight white teeth which must have cost him a small fortune.

"I understand," he said, holding out his hands as wide as his grin, "about misunderstandings. That's all we had. Nothing a phone call wouldn't clear up. I could have apologized, made things right. My boys, they're real corporate ladder climbing types. They like to impress the boss. They like to get things done. Sometimes they get excited, maybe take things too far. That's why I have to be the boss, why I have to think big picture. They have no subtly, no art. Do you understand me?"

"There's a preschool down the road. They teach all levels of finger painting."

Tancredi shook his head, let his hands fall to his side. "Brogan, you have to understand. I'm the boss, but just because I'm the boss, doesn't mean I don't work. I have a job to do just like everybody else. Lou's place is part of a bigger picture, and part of my job is making sure everyone else sees the big picture. You understand me?"

"You need to draw a new picture, one that doesn't involve Lou's place. There's other plots of land out there. Why don't you convert a strip mall? I hate those places."

"You're funny, Brogan. This isn't about strip malls. Think bigger, think taller. Think about all those zeroes which make living so much easier. I got bills, I got pressures, so I want those zeros. Hell, I *need* those zeros, but I'm also willing to share too."

His smile widened. "My bosses want results and I'm a results kind of guy. Since I'm a man of my word I have to deliver on my promises. Like everybody else, I'm just trying to climb the corporate ladder."

I said nothing.

The two henchmen had circled around quietly to either side of me. Maybe they understood the conversation, maybe they didn't. They understood one thing for certain: The boss was angry and I was the cause. They got paid to make the boss happy and when the boss wasn't happy, maybe they could break a guy's leg and put a smile back on the boss's face. Everybody's happy but the poor bastard with a broken leg.

Screw drivers, wrenches and a blow torch were within arm's reach. The blowtorch wouldn't do any good without a spark, and they would be on me by the time I found one. The wrenches were solid if swung hard enough. As long as neither man brought out a gun, I might have a chance. They were big guys, bruisers, and I thought it unlikely. They looked the type to hurt you up close and personal.

"Do you want to do this, Tancredi?" I asked. "Once I take

out your men, I'm coming after you."

His face flushed and the wide smile disappeared. He was the guy you respected or he cut you. His definition of respect was a sharp knife. He understood fear and control and extracted it through pain. You don't earn respect through pain, though, no matter how deep the cut, and in Tancredi's eyes I could see he understood this.

Tancredi's face relaxed, the anger dissolved. The transformation was almost instantaneous. "Look, let's be friends, shall we? You're a real artist. What you did other day, that was artwork and will end up in a medical journal with a big splashy photo. You make art like that for me, the world will be a better place. What do you say?"

The men eased in nonchalantly closer. Neither one went for a gun. They planned on enjoying this. They'd have fun and talk about it later, talk about how they'd heard bones break and laugh while describing the damage they'd done to my body.

The left one was within range. In a movement, the wrench was in my hand hitting him across the neck. Unable to breath, he clutched at his throat and made a burping sound. Thick fingers wrapped around his windpipe trying ineffectually to open it back up.

His partner was faster but too heavy, more used to having his targets tied to a chair, not flying in front of them. I swung the wrench around, but it went wide and sparked off the toolbox. He must have had grappling training because he moved in close and clenched at me with both hands. I'd seen that kind of work in prison, and from a Brazilian I knew how to bring my legs up into the other guy's gut. I did the move now, but it did little to slow him; his body was covered in too much fat. It did however let him get in closer. He changed tactics and squeezed his thumbs into my collar bone dropping me to my knees. With his body over me, he pushed down and if he continued, he'd have the bones broken and me sprawled out on the floor. I brought the wrench up into his groin and the pressure stopped and I fell backwards trying to catch my breath.

Tancredi laughed and when I turned around, he was clapping his hands. "You're good," he said. "You didn't hesitate, jumped right in there."

He turned as the side door opened and Munroe came through with his gun out.

Tancredi waved at him. "Hello, officer. Can we help you?"

"What the hell is going on here?"

"We were testing a new security system. Can we help you with something?"

"Back away, both of you."

Tancredi's henchmen stepped around the car and leaned against the wall, their faces flushed, their hands visible so Munroe could see them.

Tancredi faced Munroe. "Funny you showing up here like this, *detective*."

Munroe frowned at him. "I'm following up on some property damage complaints from last week. You wouldn't happen to anything about that, would you, Tancredi?"

"I'm happy to see you heeding my suggestion about not harassing good solid upstanding citizens. These streets are rough enough, would hate to see anything worse happen to the good officers of this city." He buttoned up his coat. "Sorry, I can't help you. I don't get over to this side of town much. All the crime, you know."

Tancredi turned towards me. "I'm looking forward to further conversations with you."

He stepped out the door and the two men followed him.

"I could have taken him out," I said.

Munroe said, "They would have killed you."

"I need to talk to Kelly."

NINETEEN

"I'll take you over there," Munroe said.

"I'll take a taxi."

"Do you have any of my money left?"

I considered. After giving Julian the money, the bar, the taxi ride over there and the ride back home, I couldn't buy a meal at the diner let alone get to Kelly's house. "I want to talk to him alone."

"We'll discuss that on the way."

I turned off the space heaters, made notes about the Ford and closed the shop.

"Lou gave you a key?"

"No. Julian showed me where they keeps the spare."

"Where is he?"

"In the hospital. Tancredi's men did a number on him."

Munroe climbed into the driver's seat and started the engine, while I got in on the passenger side.

"I'm sorry," he said. "Is he a good guy?"

"I gave him the last of your money."

"Well, that was dumb. Nobody's that good."

He pulled out of the parking lot and put us onto the highway, into Friday afternoon traffic.

I watched the city go by, while thinking about Sam. The last time we spoke, I felt something I wanted to hold for the rest of my life. We shared a spark of hope for a future where we would wake up in the middle of the night and experience peace in finding the other there. We could have a future without this city. A future somewhere with mountains and trails and a dog.

"Why you smiling?" Munroe asked.

"I imagined you getting promoted to captain. It's a life's dream of mine."

"Go to hell."

Lou's house was a two-story brick place squished between two others. Shoveled driveways lined the street, except Kelly's. His sat under a foot of snow. Tire tracks cut through stopping at a garage set off from the house. A wooden gate blocked by snow stood half open giving entry to a small backyard.

"Is he home?" Munroe asked.

"Yes."

"Think he booby trapped the place?"

"You mean with claymores in the backyard and punji sticks along the sidewalk? Seriously?"

"Probably not."

"Probably not," I repeated.

We got out of the car. Our breath puffed in the evening air.

"I've seen vets doing stranger things," he continued. "One guy tried mounting a machine gun turret in his front yard. He figured if he put up enough camouflage netting, nobody would notice. You do that in the suburbs, people tend to notice."

"Where you get this stuff?"

Munroe shrugged. "People are crazy."

We walked through the snow up to the front door in the dark. Thick blinds covered the windows.

"No mail," I said.

"Who gets mail anymore?"

I rang the doorbell and waited. No sound came from the house.

"Knock on the door," Munroe said impatiently.

I wanted to tell him to wait in the car. I didn't need him causing trouble with Kelly, but I said nothing and knocked on the door. A minute passed, and I knocked again. I heard noises from inside this time: the big gray dog barked and a snapped command from Kelly quieting him.

Kelly opened the door holding a sawed-off shotgun and chomping on a cigar. "I'm not happy to see you."

Munroe waved from behind me. "Howdy, Lou."

"Now, I'm not happy to see either one of you. You're a couple of sucking chest wounds."

I didn't know what that meant, so I asked, "Can we come in?"

Kelly stepped back and Munroe and I funneled into a dark room. We waited by the door, until Kelly flipped a switch on a floor lamp. We stood in a box of a living room containing a reclining chair with an end table next to it, a round dog bed, an unused fireplace and a bookshelf lining one wall.

"That coffee brewing?" Munroe asked.

Kelly nodded. "Why the hell you here?"

Munroe coughed. "We wanted to see how you were doing."

"Takes two of you? Why didn't you call?"

"Can we go into the kitchen?" I asked.

"I'm a cop, right? Can you put away the shotgun, please?" Munroe asked.

Kelly scowled at him, but stopped at a broom closet on the way to the kitchen and placed the shotgun on a shelf. Several boxes of shotgun shells sat on a shelf below it.

In the kitchen, Munroe poured himself a cup of coffee and stood against the counter. I sat at the table. Kelly sat across from me.

"What's going on?" Kelly asked.

"Tancredi showed up today."

"So?" His eyes narrowed, looking at me. "Your face is a combination plate of beets and mashed potatoes. How many fights you been in?"

Munroe sipped his coffee grinning.

"Tell me about Tancredi," I said.

Kelly scowled. "You're a son of a bitch."

I went to the coffee pot and made myself a cup. I didn't want coffee, but I wanted to give him time to pull himself together.

I put the cup on the table.

He frowned at me and bit harder on his cigar. "Have a cup."

Under the kitchen light he looked old, but not disheveled. His eyes looked at me slightly fuzzy, but not asleep, not drunk. He wore a green t-shirt, brown khakis and quality walking shoes. Not good in the snow, but he wasn't going outside.

Kelly looked at Munroe. "Why'd you bring him here?"

"He asked me to."

"You're both sons of bitches."

Munroe disappeared around the corner back into the living room. Cupboards opened and closed and I heard the flick of a light and darkness. Munroe came back. "The dog upstairs?"

"Yeah, he's in my room with my other shotgun."

"Fine, Lou," Munroe said. "I'll back off."

"Julian is in the hospital," I said. "The men who tore up the shop put him there."

Kelly pulled the cigar from his mouth, set it on the table. He looked at his hands, flexed his scarred fingers. "He stuck it out when everyone else left. I didn't blame them, there was nothing worth staying for, but he stayed. Last couple years been rough. It's gotten so I can't run an honest business. That leads to the kind of stress a guy at my age can't handle, but he helped me out just by staying." He looked up. "How's his wife?"

"She's keeping it together."

Kelly shook his head. "He never shut up about her, the dumb kid."

"You missed work," I said.

Kelly took a deep breath, exhaled it. He glanced at Munroe, then at me. "I'm retiring. I don't have it in me anymore."

"Retiring?" Munroe asked. "What the hell are you talking about? Where did this come from?"

I gave him a look to shut him up, but he ignored me.

"Explain yourself," Munroe continued. "I've put a ton of hours into your case. We got this cracked. You can't retire because you're tired!"

"No, not that. Maybe that. I was in the hospital. The doctors they did tests. I got cancer. The doctors said I still look healthy, could run five miles if I wanted, but they said I got two months or maybe one if I'm lucky. It's eaten up most of my insides. The docs are all aflutter, because they're baffled why I'm still walking."

He wiped tears away from his eyes. Munroe handed him a

dish towel.

Kelly said, "There ain't much worse than a doctor staring at you ready to pounce. Swear I saw one holding a carving knife. He was waiting for me to die so he could cut me open. It's gruesome. You're not a person anymore, just a curiosa in a freak show."

"That where you been the last couple of days?"

"That and talking to a lawyer. If I sell the shop, Tancredi will get it. I won't let that happen. Anybody I give it to will get leaned on hard enough they'll end up in the hospital. I can't do that to anybody, not to you, not to Julian. The lawyer said, if I don't want Tancredi to get it, the best thing to do is to leave a mess of paperwork he can't untangle. My last sorry attempt at stopping him after all he's done to me."

"Do you think it will work?" I asked.

"The lawyer said it could take two years or it could take ten. Tancredi won't wait that long. He can't wait that long. His backers won't let him."

"Why didn't you sell to him?"

"He offered me piles of money, each one bigger than the last. By the end, he was near crazy yelling at me to take it. The funny thing was, if he'd come at me soft, I would have considering selling but he didn't. He came in with thugs and guns and threats."

"I reiterated your position to him."

Kelly grinned. "Reiterated, huh? I would have liked to have seen that. And he didn't hurt you."

"He didn't hurt me."

"He's committed to somebody with money and they're forcing his hand so he's fighting in the open now. You need to be careful."

Lou picked up a lighter and rolled the cigar around the flame. "I quit smoking cigars twenty years ago, because the wife didn't care for the smell. Gave her headaches. But not a day went by I didn't crave one." He shook his head. "Two days ago, I got permission to stop worrying about my health. I can eat what I want, drink what I want, and smoke what I want." He frowned. "I think I'd rather have carrots and another twenty years."

Munroe set his coffee mug on the counter. "I'll be outside."

We watched him go out the backdoor and stand in the cold dark.

"You know," Kelly said. "I figured we would have solved the cancer thing by now since so many people like to smoke. Sure, it's a dirty habit, but there's something good about it too, something calming and simple. Helps a guy think through a problem. Or when you see two strangers strike up a conversation on a street corner when one of them bums a smoke. The world needs more of that. Peace over a cigarette."

"You want to share a cigarette with Tancredi?"

Kelly growled, "Some folks don't share well."

"Tell me who he's involved with."

Kelly picked up his cigar and lit it with a lighter from his pocket. He took several puffs, filling his mouth with smoke. The gray ash he knocked off into the tray. "Let's sit on the back porch. It's not as warm but smoking in the house makes me feel guilty towards my wife's memory."

I followed him to the porch out the side of the house and sat on a chair. Kelly sat across from me. The room was more sunroom than porch.

"Tancredi," I repeated, seeing my breath.

Kelly fussed around for another minute, and finally sighed. "He's been after the shop for a good three years. The trouble started small, with simple things like intimidating my customers, but never outright and never at the shop. Simple suggestions like they should go to other places to get their work done. Only, the last three months he dropped any kind of pretense and beat my customers. He had one of his guys crack an old timer on the head, and it put him in the hospital for a week. Insurance company dropped me, the city revoked my license."

Munroe came in and leaned against the doorframe.

"He set up protests outside the shop, claimed one customer didn't get any work done to his automobile. They started a legal case against me. When that wasn't enough, he brought in the heavies. They beat up my last two mechanics. One of them ended up in a cast."

I turned to Munroe. "Russians."

Munroe nodded.

Still looking at Munroe, I said, "Which is why you put me there. You figured you'd solve two problems at once."

Munroe nodded again.

"You gotta understand, Johnny, he was only trying to take the heat off me. We figured, if you could help, I could keep the shop going."

"You expected me to go after Tancredi."

"It's what you do," Munroe said. "We put a camera on a car to catch Tancredi or one of his men vandalizing it, but they never touched it. Somebody told them to leave it alone."

"A cop?"

Munroe nodded. "I tried to root them out with no luck. Every step of the way we met resistance. Didn't matter at what level. Tancredi had money and he spent it wisely."

"My business is done. Those two cars sitting in the bays, they're it. The last work I'll ever get. Nobody will come within five blocks of the place."

"What do you expect me to do?" I asked.

Lou stood up, pointed the hot cigar at me. "I expect you to kill him. I expect you to walk up to him and knock his god damn block off. I expect you to put him out of his misery so I won't lose everything."

"I won't do that."

He punched his finger into my chest. I could feel the hot coal of the cigar in his hand. "I thought you were something but you're nothing. You're a bum just like the rest of them."

"He's a cop," I said, pointing at Munroe, "Have him do his job. Arrest Tancredi."

"We've arrested him several times," Munroe said, "but he owns the courts. You heard him before. We go at him again, cops die."

"When civilization goes to hell," Kelly said, "it goes fast. There's no slow lane because men like Tancredi grease the street with blood."

"You want me to walk up to him and kill him execution style."

"After what's he's done, yes," Kelly said, his eyes steady. "Smack him around first, make everyone know that route's going to hurt in the only way that matters."

"Killing him solves nothing," I said. "because where does it end? I kill Tancredi, then what? Somebody else takes his place. How many Tancredi's are there in the world? It's the same thing happened with Boris Egorov: I killed him and within a week the cocaine flowed again. A lot of guys are willing to take his place for the money and the power."

"You kill him, the rats hesitate. If another one pops up, you kill him. You keep killing the bastards until they get smart, until they realize they need to stop. It's the only way."

"Has he killed anyone?" I asked.

"No," Munroe said. "But it's only a matter of time."

"I'll slap a guy around if he deserves it. I won't kill a man because he manipulated a corrupt legal system," I said.

"No, I suppose you won't." Kelly turned to Munroe. "Get him out of here. I got little enough time to live, I don't want to spend it looking at him."

"You seriously asking me to kill Tancredi?"

Kelly put his head in his hands. "I don't know what to do anymore. I'm out of options, kid."

I put my hand on his shoulder. "We'll figure something out."

TWENTY

"Where am I taking you?" Munroe asked.

I told him the name of the diner where Sam worked. He put the car in drive and we rode in silence. He didn't smoke or cough. He made the smallest possible movements to navigate the car through city traffic.

Twenty minutes later he pulled us into the diner parking lot, his face pale and his eyes wet with fatigue. He needed sleep, but he wouldn't get any soon.

"We shouldn't have asked you to do that," he said.

"It's the right play if he's as bad as you think he is." I sighed. "But all he's done so far is harass Kelly and scare off a few customers."

"He had Julian beat up."

"Is that enough to kill a guy?"

Munroe shook his head. "Guess not."

"We know he's going to do worse. We have to catch him before it can't be undone."

"Before he kills someone."

"Before he kills someone."

"Who's the cop here?" Munroe asked.

"Not me," I said. "I can't carry a gun."

I got out of the car and he drove away. I took a deep breath, exhaled and watched the cloud dissolve in the bitter air. Shadows filled the corners of the parking lot making it feel cramped. I imagined walking into the diner, seeing Sam and saying *hello*; hearing her response in her quiet voice. Then we smile at one another, lean in for a hug, her lavender scent comforting me.

I hesitated at the door. My temples throbbed and my eyes itched, but she didn't need my troubles added to her own so I took several deep breaths before walking inside.

The woman behind the cash register smiled as I approached her.

"Sam around?" I asked.

Her smile stayed pleasant, but she shook her head. "She's not working tonight."

I paused, looked around the restaurant as if I'd find her, nodded and said, "She doesn't work Friday nights?"

"Sometimes."

"The best night to get tips, right?"

"It is."

"Thanks," I said.

She continued her pleasant smile, as I turned around and walked outside. The air felt colder, harsher now that I had to walk eight blocks to Sam's house. I put on my cap and gloves and pulled up my collar. I headed east, walking as fast as I could without slipping and falling on the ice.

I stopped after two blocks to knock snow from my boots on a light pole. The cigarette-stain yellow light turned my coat and boots gray and spotlighted me on the empty street. I looked to both ends, saw nothing, and continued walking.

I found Sam's place, squeezed between an entire block of

identically painted single story houses, after doubling back twice. I only recognized it because the neighbor's car still sat in the driveway.

I rang the doorbell wondering if I had made a mistake coming unannounced, but when the door opened and Sam stood before me I knew I needed this woman and the hour could be damned. She wore a pair of dark jeans and a cashmere sweater with a button up shirt underneath. The shirt, white and crisp, wasn't what I expected from the woman I met at the diner. This was a different animal.

"You weren't always a waitress, were you?"

"No," she said.

"May I come in?"

"Are you playing games with me?"

"I'm too tired for games."

She stepped back and stopped in the center of the living room. I grabbed her wrist. She stiffened, staring at me with cool blue eyes, and waited. I waited too, not releasing my hold. Her arm went limp, and I pulled her close, feeling her breath on my lips. I encircled her in my arms and kissed her. She cried out, bit at me hungrily and brought her leg up around mine.

"I missed you too," I said.

She leaned her head against my chest. "When you didn't call, I ridiculed myself for caring about you. I wouldn't even look in the mirror I got so disappointed."

"Three days," I said.

"Three days is three years when it comes to making a fool of yourself worrying."

"I'm sorry," I said.

She searched my face for some false emotion, some subterfuge and when she didn't find it she pushed me towards the couch. "Sit."

I sat while she walked to the kitchen, glancing back to make sure I was still there. She returned with two open beers, handed me one and took a drink of her own.

"Talk to me," she said.

I thought about how to approach the conversation with Kelly, how to essentialize the last couple of days and found no way to untangle it all in a way that would make sense without a lot of explaining. "I was asked to kill a man today."

"Oh."

I took a swig of my beer, watched her processing what I said.

"You're not joking."

"I'm not joking."

She looked at her beer bottle. "Guess it would depend upon who asked and why. Whatever answer you give, it wouldn't be simple."

"I said no. I couldn't do it, not like they asked."

"Are service mechanics frequently called on to do such things?"

"I didn't lie to you. I do work on cars."

While she thought about this, I walked to the bookshelf and picked up the framed copy of her engineering degree.

"I worked eight hard years to get that degree," she said. "My father offered to help, but I did it myself. Earning that piece of paper was the proudest day of my life. Things didn't go according to plan, of course, so now I deliver plates of food."

"It's honest work."

"Honest, yes. Pays the bills, no."

"Did you work for your father?"

"For a while." She paused. "Can we skip the past? It tells us where we were and what we did, not where we want to go and who we want to be. I'm alive and so are you."

"Can we have those chops now?"

"You changing the subject?"

"I'm rusty," I said. "I'm not good at this kind of intimacy."

"You're honest, at least. But before we do, can you finish telling me what happened?"

"It's in the past."

She smiled. "Yesterday is not in the past."

I returned her smile. "I'll talk. You cook."

We walked into the kitchen. She pulled a foil covered bowl from the refrigerator and set it on the counter.

"You expecting company?" I asked.

"I prepared them two days ago. I figured if you didn't come tonight I'd eat them by myself."

I sat at the table and sipped my beer. Watching her move around the kitchen was a delight I appreciated even more than last time. Last time had been the first time: fresh, new, overwhelming. This time I felt relaxed, easy, able to take in her subtle movements, the angle of her back, the way she bent forward while working.

"Talk," she said.

"A criminal named Tancredi is trying to steal my boss's property. Tancredi scared away all the customers and sent men to damage the place."

"This is the vandals you interrupted the other night?"

I nodded. "The conflict is escalating, though. It started with harsh words, moved to fist fighting, but it's about to turn into gunplay. My boss is a cranky old vet who, I found out today, has cancer. I think he's baiting Tancredi to kill him— suicide by criminal."

"Who asked you to kill who?"

"My boss asked me to kill Tancredi."

"That doesn't sound like suicide."

"He didn't expect me to say yes."

"So, he's pushing this man to kill him. Does he have insurance?"

"He said the business is uninsured because of what Tancredi's done."

"How long did the doctors give him?"

"A month or two."

She put her hand on my arm. "I'm sorry, Johnny."

I shrugged. "I barely know the guy. But I like him. He's set up in a terrible situation. No decent way out."

She continued cooking. I stood, paced the kitchen, moved into the living room when I caught her worried looks. I glanced through the titles on her bookshelf and paced some more. I couldn't sit and I didn't want to stand. I wanted to put my fist into something, through someone who deserved it. And, damn it, part of me didn't even want to be *here* any longer. I wanted to be away, far away.

Walking back to the bookshelf, I scanned the titles again until I found one about living in the mountains. I flipped through the pages reading about planting crops and capturing rainwater to nourish them.

Lost in the idea, I heard the clink of plates on the table. I put the book down and made myself useful in the kitchen by placing silverware and napkins. After two more trips from stove to counter we had a good-sized spread laid out on the table: salad, green beans and pork chops three inches thick.

"To pork chops and mountain retreats," I said, raising my beer.

She glanced towards the living room, smiled and touched her bottle to mine.

The chops were juicy and the green beans were slathered in real butter the way I like them. We ate in silence. Finishing mine, I made a fake play for a chunk of her chop, but she deflected my fork with her knife and smiled. "You can have my scraps if I leave any," but she didn't. Afterward I cleaned up and settled next to her on the couch. She curled herself up under my arm.

"You didn't ask why I was in prison."

"I don't care for the past."

I thought again of the photo in the garage and it being an odd place to hang it. I nodded.

"Do you need to tell me?" she asked.

I leaned in, smelled her hair. She had showered before I arrived. Maybe because of me, maybe not. I took a deep breath and said, "I killed a man in self-defense and his brother wants revenge."

She remained silent for a while. "The police let you out of prison, you're free, you could go away."

"He has money and connections. I wouldn't get far. The cops believe he'll be here next week—maybe earlier. He wants me dead and he wants to do it."

"So, while some man is hunting you, you sit on my couch smelling my hair."

"You smell good."

"Thanks."

"Want me to barricade myself in the bathroom with a shotgun?"

She sat up, turned and faced me. "*We* could leave."

"Nuts," I said. "Go where? I told you, he has money. He has the cops. Wherever we go, he finds us. That's the way it works."

"I have money saved."

"Good," I said. "Use it when you need it."

"Do you need it?"

"No. I don't need or want your money."

"But if you need it, you'll ask, right?"

"Probably not," I said.

She leaned back into my arms where I felt her tension. Gradually she relaxed and I could hear her soft breathing. I turned the television on with the remote and muted the volume. Images flickered passed, but nothing could take my attention away from listening to Sam. Each rising breath a fragile sound matched with an energetic exhale.

She touched me, her fingers a soft breeze across my arm. Quiet murmurs escaped her, mumbled words, broken sleep thoughts.

The unwatched television changed shows. I thought she was asleep when she asked, "Are you happy?"

"As happy as I can be."

"Me too. Is it too early to make wishes?"

"Maybe for the ones that can come true."

"This one can't. I wish my father were alive. I'd want him to meet you."

I savored the respect she granted me by telling me this. Then I said, "You sure about that? Fathers see things different than the daughters. For one, they notice a guy's felony prison time."

"He would have liked you. His favorite hobby outside architecture was working on his motorcycles. He had two of them. When I was young, he took me on week-long road trips."

I turned Sam's face up to mine and said, "Sweetheart, you have to look hard at me because I'm not what you think I am, not by a long shot. Whatever you were, whatever that life was, it sounds damn good, but I'm not the guy who fits into that world. I break things, I don't build them. I thought I could change that when I got out, I trained for it, I hammered it into my head, but it didn't work. The minute I got out, the first thing I did was fight. I'm not pretty, I'm not soft. I'm hard and mean, and I'm not one to take home to your father. Not now or ever."

She wrapped her arms around my neck and planted a big kiss on my lips. The kiss was breathless and hard and I had to pull her back to breathe.

"You do what you have to do," she said. "I wish I could have done what you're doing now. Maybe my father would be alive today if we had been stronger." She laid her head in my lap. "He owned one of the largest construction companies in the city. That kind of business is corrupt. With the unions, the politicians, the payoffs and the scams, he couldn't stay clean. He tried, but they went after him because they couldn't buy him. They wore him down, like they're doing to your boss. I worked for him as an engineer, but I couldn't, or didn't, do anything to help. I didn't know what to do."

After a while I felt her shaking with tiny sobs. I put my hand on her shoulder. She looked at me with bloodshot eyes. "He was contracted to build a high-rise hotel downtown. He liked to walk the beams, he said it was the only way he could see the work or clear his head. He liked feeling the wind that high over the city. Dad was in construction all his life and he could climb anything. He didn't fall, he was thrown. They murdered him. Then, claiming mismanagement, they went after the company. They claimed cheap materials were used, that my father chiseled them, that he'd committed suicide because he knew he was about to be caught. They took his company, they destroyed his name and the lawyers got the last of our money."

I ran my fingers through her hair and felt the dampness of her tears on my leg. I stroked her hair until her breath became slow and even. I dozed in and out, occasionally touching her hair and drifting back to sleep.

I woke suddenly. The room was quiet. Sam slept on my

lap, my hand on her shoulder. On the television a reporter, wearing a heavy winter coat with snow on her shoulders, talked silently into the camera. The cameraman panned to the left showing four buildings in a row all burning. The one closest had a sign: *Kelly's Body Shop*.

TWENTY-ONE

When I sat forward Sam woke and asked groggily, "What's the matter?"

"Kelly's shop burned. Where's your keys?"

Sam stood up, shook out her hair and went for her coat. "I'll drive you."

"I'll take the car."

"You don't have a license."

We stumbled into the kitchen together. She picked up the keys, saw my face and handed them over. "Be careful."

I kissed her and ran out the door.

The car stayed steady on the road even though I drove much faster than the worn tires should have allowed. I made good time and pulled Sam's car up to the curb a block from Kelly's shop. The precaution proved unnecessary. The cops milled around the crowd paying little attention to anything beyond the light of the fire.

I didn't find Kelly among the faces of strangers scowling at me as I pushed through them. The police appeared relaxed moving through the routine. The fire department extinguished the last of the flame and plunged the block into a darkness broken only by police cruisers and firetrucks. The crowd, suddenly feeling their vulnerability in the darkness, disbursed. Two EMTs watched for a sign from the Fire Marshall; when he shook his head, they climbed into their truck and drove away.

A uniformed cop sized me up from half a block away, but must have considered me not worth the effort because he closed his notebook and climbed into his cruiser.

I got back in the car and pointed it towards Kelly's house. When I arrived, I parked the car in front, ran up the steps and pounded on the door. A neighbor turned on their outside light and peered at me through a curtained window. Their dog barked, but Kelly's didn't. I waited thirty seconds before trying the door. It was unlocked.

The living room was in shambles. Someone had attacked it with knives and a bat. Gutted chairs lay on their sides; white stuffing spread across the floor. Smashed shelves, lamps and tables littered the floor like toothpicks. Nothing in the room remained untouched. Had the neighbors heard the destruction, and chosen to not respond?

I walked around the mess calling Kelly's name. No response. I stopped at the closet and saw the shotgun missing and only half the shells remaining on the shelf below. In the kitchen, contents of the cupboards and drawers were dumped on the floor. Silver and broken glass glittered under the overhead light. The refrigerator door stood open, the weak light giving the room a cheap plastic look. A dog food bowl sat turned over in one corner. I went to the stairs and listened and hearing nothing climbed them slowly.

Upstairs I found two bedrooms and a bathroom. One contained a mattress pushed off its box spring and next to it an upturned lamp casting shadows across the ceiling. The second room held a long desk and stacks of sewing materials shown to be long unused by layers of dust clinging to the containers. I didn't find Kelly's second shotgun in either room.

Kelly's truck sat cold in the garage. I walked back to the kitchen and sat at the table. So how had they gotten him? If he was upstairs with the dog, he had protection and early warning. No way the dog would allow someone into the house without barking and no way Kelly would ignore it under the circumstances. They took him out of the house without a struggle, without neighbors knowing and went to work on the place. Nothing seemed to have been taken besides the guns, which meant they damaged the house out of spite. It made no sense.

I called the police station and asked for Munroe. After a long pause, he answered.

I said, "I'm at Kelly's house. Somebody sacked the place. He's not here but his truck is in the garage. Did you hear about his shop?"

"We're working with the fire department, but it will take time to find out what happened."

"What happened is Tancredi burned it down. Can you bring him in?"

Phones rang and people talked in the background. After a pause he said, "I don't want to do that."

"Why not?"

"We need something on him he can't make disappear with money or connections."

"We need to catch him. *You* need to catch him. You get him and I'll take over after that."

"He'll have an alibi."

"I don't care about alibis."

"Even if we grab him, he won't tell us anything."

"He'll talk to me."

"I thought you didn't want to go there."

"If Kelly is alive, he'll have a chance at living."

"I don't understand why he would grab Lou tonight. It's Friday. Tancredi can't do anything with the property until Monday. Sitting on Lou doesn't gain him anything."

"He burned the shop down out of revenge."

"That puts him at risk," Munroe said.

"With who? He's got the courts and Russian money. Kelly caused him all kinds of trouble and he's mad about it. Why wouldn't he grab him, work him over and have him broken and ready to sign the paperwork come Monday? Tuesday he owns the place. Then, the property is his and Kelly is dead."

"I'll see what I can do. We'll start with a list of places he might be. I can put two guys on this, but nothing else yet. We need proof he was involved. I need a witness, something that connects him. Without it, if we put pressure on him, he's liable to go after the cops."

"You think he can do that?"

"Yes, Brogan, I think he can. He has the money and the firepower."

"Arrest him and get me in a room with him."

"You can't touch him if we have him in custody."

"Find him, arrest him, let him loose. I'll know where he is. I'll talk with him."

"The department has to stay clean."

"You will."

"I'll call you back once we know something."

I hung up the phone, fished a piece of paper out of my pocket and dialed the number. The phone rang six times before Charlie answered in a low voice.

"This is Brogan," I said. "What's your address?"

Silence. Hesitation. The click of a light. I could see it all in my head: her lying in bed, sitting up and turning on the light next to her. Maybe she was naked maybe she wasn't. She looked at a clock and saw it was the middle of the night. The time registered in her head slow and sluggish. Her brain spun trying to figure out the next angle. "You—you want to see me now?"

"Stop stalling, Charlie, and give me the damn address."

She gave me the address, and I hung up.

I turned towards the front door and stopped. My head suddenly felt too heavy for my body and my eyes burned under the kitchen light. Any rest I got from sitting on Sam's couch was gone. I wanted to lie down and not have to think about things for a long time: no angles to untangle, no killers to catch, no watching friends die. I wanted sleep, a lot of it.

And I wanted Sam. I wanted Sam frying up a stack of pancakes and pork chops. I wanted her naked next to me on a cold winter morning. I wanted her in my arms, her body warm and inviting. I wanted to peer into her blue eyes.

Soon. I would get it soon. Just not yet.

TWENTY-TWO

Charlie's place turned out to be a skyscraper overlooking the river from the south. I pushed through the revolving door and entered a perfectly heated foyer with a forty-foot ceiling and a shiny waxed floor.

A lone man sitting behind a bank of monitors stood upon my approach. Clean shaven, pressed suit and a holstered gun under his left arm made him the perfect combination of manager and night security. "May I help you?"

"Charlie Adler."

"Your name, sir?"

"Brogan."

He smiled pleasantly, typed into a keyboard and we waited, two strangers trapped awkwardly together for three minutes. His face reflected a green light. He glanced at it, continued with his smile and waved me towards the bank of elevators behind him. "Elevator three. No need to press the buttons, sir. You'll arrive on your floor."

The elevator whisked me fifty-three floors into the sky and I felt none of the effort. A bell dinged, the door opened and I stepped out. Charlie's apartment stood right ahead, the door propped open with a spilled gin bottle. The contents stained the brown carpet and several wet footprints tracked across the marble foyer.

I stepped over the bottle into the apartment and found Charlie lying on the floor of the living room, her arms sprawled and her hair a wild tangled mess. She clutched the stem of a broken wineglass in her hand. The left wrist faced upwards. I could see where she'd jammed the stem into it, punctured the vein and spilled her blood as thick as wine.

I sighed, picked her up and tossed her onto the leather couch. Blood stained her pajamas, the couch, my shirt. She mumbled, the sounds so quiet the creak of the leather drowned them out. I could have thrown her out the window for all she cared. Maybe I should have.

Instead, I dug around the bathroom, a mass of chrome and marble and horribly bright lights, until I found towels, tape and gauze. In the kitchen, I filled a bowl with warm water from a sink as big as a bathtub. I brought everything back to the living room and set it on the table next to her.

The wound wasn't deep, but she'd mashed the veins good. I took my time cleaning away the blood, careful to make sure no glass remained. Layers of pink scars ran along both wrists. I wrapped her wrist carefully in loose gauze and taped it in place. I turned her on her side, the bandaged arm in front of her and waited until she began to snore.

The apartment was glass, chrome and leather. Two bedrooms opened off a long hallway. One room she slept in, the other she used as a dressing room. Both rooms had closets full of dresses, coats and shoes. Angled furniture, expensive and unfriendly, filled every room. Whatever her choices, she lived in money now.

I finished my tour and sat in a chair across from her so she would see me when she woke. Asleep she appeared peaceful, the idealized portrait of a sophisticated woman in respite. Red silk pajamas worn over smooth fresh washed skin, and her hair spilling over a green down pillow made her appear almost lovable. But the pajamas hid blood stains, and the green matched too close the envy in her. Unseen in the portrait were the twelve long years ending in tonight.

I briefly remembered enjoying her. She contained a spontaneity sadly lacking in most of humanity. You never had a dull day with Charlie around. But going to prison was the clarity I needed. I was a satellite to her supernova. Even now it burned me, causing me to second guess every decision. I didn't understand her power when we were young. Youth creates its own insanity. Decisions so seemingly healthy appear downright suicidal ten years later. We were two hungry kids finding our place in the world, but now...I rubbed my eyes feeling tired and old. I watched her fingers twitch into fists in her sleep. I considered her life now. What twists and turns got her to this cage high in the sky? Where would I be if I hadn't gone to prison?

I took a deep breath. No, I didn't miss her. I missed being young and Charlie was a part of that. The past swam before me.

When I woke, Charlie sat at the window overlooking the city. A glass of water and a bottle of pills sat next to her and when I stirred, she shivered.

"You trying again?" I asked.

She looked at the pill bottle. "They're pain relief. My wrist hurts."

"They taught us about suicide in prison. People try for five main reasons. There's depression, the most common reason. Not surprising considering the number of men incarcerated for life. Puts a damper on your thinking in ways it's hard to imagine. You depressed, Charlie?"

"No."

"Good. The second reason is they're psychotic. This manifests itself as voices. Do you hear voices telling you to do things?"

Charlie laughed. "You're crazy, Johnny. You had way too much time to think screwy thoughts in prison."

"The third reason, now that sounds like you: impulsive. People get drunk and try to off themselves because they run down a dark path and can't find themselves a way out. Did that happen tonight?"

Charlie touched her bandaged wrist and looked out the window for a long time. "No, Johnny, I always find my way back."

"The fourth reason is a cry for help. You crying for help?"

Charlie shook her head, remained silent.

"Do you have a terminal disease?"

She smiled sadly. "Does love count?"

"Why are you stabbing yourself with a wine glass?"

"Come sit with me. Look on the city."

I stood beside her and watched her in the window's reflection.

"I missed this place," she said. "I would turn the lights low and watch the river every night. A thick black line cutting the city in two. Here the last remnants of society. There's the hope of a future I'll never see. So many lights over there. I wondered if they saw me looking out my window. Do they know I'm here?"

"Why don't you go there?"

"This place isn't mine. It's where he keeps us. We rotate out. He doesn't live here and neither do we, but we have to stay here when it's our turn. I have my own little apartment in a complex behind a strip mall. You can look out the window and see the sign pointing out of town—can reach out and touch it. Nobody there knows who I am. They call me Cindy. It's nice not being me. The past no longer weighs on me. The future is in front of me and Cindy can chase it."

I waved my hand at this place. "Tancredi gives you money, sell everything in this place, the clothes alone would buy you a car. Take the money and leave town."

She shook with a short laugh. "I walked to the bridge once right after you went to prison. The wind nearly knocked me over, but I made it to the top, then I couldn't go on. The river flowed black and fast below me. It mesmerized me. I thought about climbing the railing and jumping in, ending it all right there. But I couldn't. Not without you."

"You're lying now."

"No, it's true. I couldn't get over you. I tried to visit. I tried to apologize. I wrote letters and never sent them. Then one day I met a girl and then a guy and somewhere along the way I got connected to Tancredi. Now I watch the bridge from here wondering if one day I'll try again."

She turned and faced me, her body small and frail. She touched her wrist. "You saved me. After everything you've said, you still saved my life. I don't know how to say I'm sorry."

"Tancredi built a hell of cage for his beautiful bird. Where is he?"

"Do you think I'm beautiful?"

"It was an expression."

She nodded. She sipped the water. "It's going to get nasty, isn't it, Johnny?"

"The best thing to do is accept it."

"You're a real bastard, Johnny."

"You were on the path to redemption."

"There's no redemption for me." She laughed, cynical and

bitter. "I should kill myself."

"The wine glass is on the table. I won't try to save you this time."

"You got it all figured out, don't you? You think you're smarter than the rest of us. You think we're all dummies. Well, we're not. We got brains too and you can't be smarter than all of us, not even half of us."

"I'm not smarter than anybody, Charlie. I'm here to make people pay their debts."

"What gives you the right?"

"Nothing, Charlie. Nothing gives me the right. I'm taking it."

"Maybe it was an accident? Maybe Lou brought it on himself?"

"You see a guy on the street, is he asking to be robbed because he's walking? It doesn't work that way. Tancredi has to answer for what he's done."

She fell to her knees in front of me, her arms hugging my legs. "Please, Johnny, just go! Leave us what we got. It'll be done soon. The Russians will come and they'll kill him dead. You'll get your revenge, and I'll be left with nothing."

"*Where is he?*"

"I haven't seen him in a month, honest. I got a call yesterday, told me to be here today. It was my turn, so I came. I heard rumors though. He got in with the Russians and now things are screwy. I may not see him for a week."

"Call him. Get him here."

"I can't, Johnny. I don't have a number. Nobody does. He leaves here and finds other beds to sleep in."

"Does he have other regulars?"

"No. I'm the only one he ever comes back to. The rest don't last a week. That means something, right? That says something about me, right?"

"What about your brother?"

"Roy? Roy can't help us. Tancredi hates him. They got in a fight that goes back a long time."

"Could he get to Tancredi through the Russians?"

"I don't think so. The Russians are looking for him too."

"What's going on, Charlie? What are you not telling me?"

"Nothing you don't already know."

I walked to the door.

"Johnny, stay, please? I feel safe with you around."

I took the elevator down to the main floor. I didn't have to touch any buttons. It was all automatic.

TWENTY-THREE

I left Charlie's apartment and drove to the river while doing my best to push away the thought of Sam waiting on the couch, her arms inviting, her body warm and snuggled close. She would need answers, and she deserved them, but right now I didn't want to talk. I wanted to be cold and alone and staring out at a space as empty as the hole in my chest. It was an hour before sunup and nobody else was around.

I parked the car in the lot below the bridge Charlie couldn't cross. The bridge loomed metallic and sharp against the fuzzy gold city lights reflected in the river. Green and red safety lights flashed off the black waters where tugboats drifted, dark turtles breaking through chunks of packed snow and ice.

Reflecting the broken shoreline of docks and shipping containers, the river, a half mile wide, exerted tons of pressure against rock and ice, immortal forces opposing one another in a war neither side could win.

A path ran along the river and under the bridge. The river, a long twisted snake, empty and dark, disappeared in either direction under broken streetlights and piles of dirty snow. I turned away from the bridge and walked the path south along the river. The cold cut through my numbness stabbing at the skin on my face and burning the tissue of my lungs. I walked alone: no one behind me, no one in front of me. The trail was a long, wide, flat ribbon moving endlessly in the darkness. The tugboats called to me in their low voices. I had no answer for them, I had no answer for myself.

Munroe would find Tancredi. That left me with nothing to do: no homes, no businesses, no hiding holes I could shine the light of my righteous fury upon.

I thought of two men coming from two directions.

Petr Egorov somewhere out there coming by boat or plane. Munroe had said a week or maybe two, and now that time had come. Egorov could appear at any time. Where were his men? What nastiness were they waiting to unleash?

Lou Kelly was an old man dying of cancer, who was now probably dying faster and more painfully in a dark basement getting worked over by a man wearing leather gloves. The thought made me sick, while the alternative, him being beyond having anything done to him, wouldn't square in my brain either. He couldn't be dead, not yet. Not with these bastards still breathing. I needed to find him and show him the look of my knuckles after I found Tancredi and his men.

I walked a mile or more in the snow before the sun appeared over trees and buildings, its yellowish red light flooding the sky. I turned around and started back to the car. I felt better after the walk, but I still didn't have a plan. If Kelly was dead, I would put a bullet in Tancredi the minute I found him. That wasn't a plan, though, that was a reaction. And would it solve much? Someone would be there to sit on Tancredi's throne long before his corpse was cold. It was the way of the world now. Men no longer believed working hard allowed them to achieve their dreams of a better life. Now they stood behind men like Tancredi waiting for the mistake which gave them their own time holding the whip while ignoring that another stood behind them waiting for the mistake that would give them their time.

I put the car in drive and pulled out of the lot. Luckily, traffic was light. Twice I almost closed my eyes for too long. I had to turn off the heater and roll the windows down so I didn't wrap the car around the nearest telephone pole. I left the car in Sam's driveway and stumbled to the door, ready to leave the key under her mat but the door opened.

She stood in the doorway with an oversized mug in her hands and a bathrobe pulled tight enough around her that the shape of her breasts and hips were obvious. I couldn't help but grin stupidly.

"It was a hell of a night," I said.

"I made cocoa. Have a cup and lie next to me."

She led me into the bedroom and I sat on the edge of the bed next to a stand with a lamp and clock. My vision was so fuzzy; I couldn't see the hands on the clock.

"I'll get the cocoa," she said.

"No," I said. "Come here."

I pulled her close and opened her robe. She wore only panties—a small frilly piece of cloth I could have torn off her with a tug. But I didn't because it wasn't time. Instead I kissed her belly. Her muscles tightened and a long slow breath escaped her. She pulled back and looked down with wide questioning eyes.

"Not yet," I said. "I just need to touch you."

Together we pulled my clothes off and got under the sheets where I fell instantly asleep.

We woke in the afternoon. Our lips found each other, then our hands, then our bodies pressed hard against one another.

The sheets were cool, the bedside clock the only light.

I pushed back the covers and ran my fingers between the valley of her breasts up over her neck to her face as she rose over me. Her hair spilled around us, canopying us from the world. She touched my lips, I leaned up and kissed her gently, then harder when she didn't resist. She pushed back, her hands digging into my chest, then her mouth took me in hungrily. She brought my hands to her breasts, squeezed my hands around them until the nipples hardened under the pressure. I ran my hand along her belly, down to the thin panties separating our bodies. She kicked the covers away to the floor and lay back watching me as I pulled the panties down around her thighs, over her ankles, then tossed them onto the floor. She hooked her arms around my neck and swung up, grinding her body against mine and crying out as I entered her.

Afterwards, I lay on the bed, my head propped up by a pillow, one leg stretched across the sheets and watched her with barely opened eyes as she walked into the bathroom. While she brushed her teeth, she glanced my way, raised an eyebrow and swayed her hips back and forth, her left arm leaning on the counter as the short t-shirt rose and fell exposing blue panties. I gave her a sleepy grin. When she finished, she turned off the light and a night light came on behind her. She stood in the doorway watching me silently. For the first time in my life I knew what it was to want someone and love someone at the same time. She ran her arm up the door frame giving me an impish grin as the edge of the shirt rose until her belly button appeared. Then with a quick motion she flipped the shirt up exposing her breasts.

"Now you got your look," she said, pouncing into the bed and climbing on top of me. She tossed the covers on us and wiggled in under my arm, resting her damp hair on my chest. She asked, "Is this going to work?"

"It will. I need to end a couple of relationships, but my calendar should be free next week for sure."

"You have a dark sense of humor."

"I wasn't trying to be funny."

"Does that make it better?"

"We'll work it out. We both want something good and right in our lives. We want to wake up next to each other and have somebody to reach out to in the night."

"I thought you were a tough guy."

"Maybe."

"I want you."

"I want you, too," I said, "But right now I need to make a call."

She curled herself within the sheets and watched me put on my pants. "Phone is in the kitchen."

In the kitchen, I dialed the police station and asked for Munroe.

"Where you been?" he asked.

"Sleeping. You?"

"Never heard of it. Dead people do that, I think."

"Cute. Have you found Tancredi?"

He paused. "They found a male body in the rubble at Lou's shop. Looks like they tied him to a chair, but no bullet wounds."

"Burned alive?"

"Looks that way."

"Yeah?"

"*Yeah.*"

"You think it's Lou?"

"Who else would it be?"

"You still trying to find him?"

"If by *him* you mean Tancredi, the answer is yes. We're not burying this. We're everywhere we think he could be. The bastard's smart, though. His shell companies own property all over the city. None of it in his name. He could be anywhere."

I gave him Sam's number. "You call me the minute you find him."

"Sure, boss."

I hung up, walked back into the bedroom and sat at the edge of bed. Sam leaned forward hugging me.

"Lou Kelly is dead. They burned him alive. The cops are looking for Tancredi, but don't think they'll find him."

"If you kill this man, what will it do for you?"

I thought about it. "I'll sleep better."

"That won't bring Lou back."

"It's not about that. Tancredi is a rat and, like a rat, when it gets into your house the only thing it knows is how to destroy. You can build walls and fences and traps, but those only slow the rat down. It'll find a way in because it's hungry and you can't plug every hole. So you have to kill it, because life can't be lived on the defensive."

"You said before you didn't want to kill him. We could leave and start over someplace else."

I shook my head. "I wouldn't kill him before because he was just a thug paying muscle to help make him big. He talked about partners. The word is it's the Russians. Maybe they got impatient and demanded results. He had to deliver the property or get himself killed." I squeezed her hand. "We'll leave afterwards. I have to finish this, because if I don't, they'll just come after me, after us."

"Johnny." Her voice was quiet, a whisper against my chest. "I love you. I'm not worried about you and I'm not worried about us. I'm worried about what the world can do to you. You don't scare me but what you're capable of does. There's a justice in you, the old kind, the kind that demands vengeance for wrongs. Maybe it's what I've always wanted but have been too afraid to find. You're here and I can't run away, but I'm worried."

I kissed her forehead. "I love you, too."

We laid on the bed.

"In the morning," I said, "We need to make plans to hide you. I don't want you in danger. They got Kelly you understand."

"I do."

I shook my head. "You're a hell of a woman. Four days ago, we were complete strangers."

"Not anymore. Let's get some sleep. I want to be ready for round two when that alarm goes off."

TWENTY-FOUR

Sunday morning, I woke, dressed and started breakfast while Sam slept. I made coffee, eggs and a pound of bacon. Munroe called but offered no new updates. "You want odds worse than a needle in a haystack, try finding a rat in a city," was all he had to say. I stewed over this while I put plates of food and two cups of hot coffee onto the table.

Sam came in wearing her college jersey and a pair of green panties. She rested her foot up on the chair and sat, smiled impishly at me while I appreciated her flexibility.

"Guess we're more at ease with one another," I said.

She stabbed at a piece of bacon off my plate, but I deflected her fork with a knife. She grinned. "Guess we're not *that* at ease."

"It's *bacon*," I said.

Sam frowned. "You're tense. They haven't found him."

With more frustration than I wanted to express, I said, "They haven't found him."

When we'd finished, I took the plates to the sink while she sipped her coffee.

"Then I need to leave today," she said.

I sat down across from her. "I don't know where Tancredi is. He could hit me anywhere. I don't want you involved in a gunfight."

"Where do I go?"

"As far from here as you can."

"How will you find me?"

"In a week, leave a message at the Sunshine Motel."

"Should I come back?"

"No. I'll come to you. I don't want to know where you're going and I don't want you to contact anyone you might know. They could come at anybody to get at either one of us."

"Do they know about me and where I live?"

"Not yet, but once they do you won't be safe."

"Will it end?"

"Once Tancredi is out of the picture you'll be safe. His men are loyal to his money. Without him, they have no reason to pursue us."

"Unlike the Russian."

"He's problem number two."

"I go to the range every couple of months. I'm a decent shot. I could stay and watch your back."

I shook my head. "You're a better shot than me, I'll give you that. I've used a gun once. Is killing something you can live with? It's different from range shooting. There's guts and brains and blood. Killing is messy and ugly and doesn't wash off."

She paled. "I will if I have to."

"I believe you, only I don't want you to."

"You asking or telling?"

"I'm asking. But I'm asking for the same reason I don't think men and women should be in combat together, *especially* men and women who sleep together."

"That's sexist."

"Probably. But I'm not going to debate you. The thought of you getting shot or killed makes me sick. I couldn't function like I need to knowing you could get hurt."

"Would it help if I said I wouldn't get shot?"

I laughed and pulled her into my arms.

She began crying. I petted her hair until the sobs became silent shivers.

"You're asking me to live with the unknown," she said. "You're asking me to go away without knowing if you're alive and without knowing if you'll return to me. I'm going to worry about a call which may never come."

"Your job is harder than mine. I just have to worry about being shot."

Her bright blue eyes watched me intently. "Or killed. I don't want to lose you."

I said nothing.

"There's a gun in the cupboard. It's older than my father, but it's accurate. If you don't need it, I'll take it. I've carried it before and know how to hide it. Anybody comes after me, I'll use it if I must."

I grinned and scooped her up in my arms. "I'm going to marry you."

She smiled through thin lips. "One thing at a time, Johnny Brogan. Let's start with going back to bed. I want dessert."

She took me into the bedroom and we undressed and made love. It was slow and passionate and we took our time, neither saying anything, but using our hands and our bodies to express our thoughts. Afterwards we slept in one another's arms. Later that night she left the room and returned with the gun and put it on the nightstand.

"Just in case," she said.

I picked up the gun, a Smith and Wesson .357. It weighted little more than a pound and held five rounds. I fumbled with the release and looked at the five bullets in the cylinder. New bullets stamped with *.357 MAG* around the edge of the brass case. I closed the cylinder and put the gun back on the nightstand. "Just in case."

I tore off a small pile of bills from my pocket and had Sam show me a place to hide the money in her closet. She took some money from her purse and added it to the hidden pile. "Just in case."

The rest of the evening Sam packed, made plans and occasionally hugged or kissed me. We didn't speak. Intermittently she would stop, take a deep breath and continue packing. Later, I found her crying on her bed. Through her tears she asked, "What about the house? The furniture. All of my stuff."

"Hire someone to sell everything."

Her jaw clenched, and she shook. "Am I insane? I'm leaving my house, my job, everything I've ever cared about for a man I met only a week ago. You're involved with criminals, people are being murdered. Everything I know says I should run away from you."

"I want you in my life, Sam, but you're taking a huge risk being involved with me. I understand if you choose to go your own way, but no matter what you do, you need to hide for a couple of weeks. Afterwards, I'll respect whatever decision you make."

"I want you in my life. I just—I just wanted a simple life."

"We'll start simplifying in the morning. For now, let's get some sleep."

TWENTY-FIVE

We awoke the next morning packed and ready to leave. Over a final cup of coffee, a knock at the door startled us both. Sam took the gun from her purse, handed it to me, and went to the door. She waited until I positioned myself beside the couch with a clear view out the front window. I could see a man standing at the doorway. I nodded and Sam opened the door. Roy Adler rubbed his nose and waved at Sam like they were old friends. He leaned in and looked at me. "Hey, Brogan. What's up?"

I pointed the gun at him. "What are you doing here?"

He smiled. "What kind of piece is that?"

"What do you want?" I asked.

"A revolver, right? It's the girl's gun. Probably belonged to her father. I bet it's ancient. But a revolver is a good home defense piece. Less chance of failure."

"Last time," I said.

He put his hands up in mock arrest. "Hey, don't shoot. I'm just a cop in this city. I'm Roy Adler," he said, putting his hand out to Sam.

She looked at me, waiting.

"Wow," Adler said, "You two are made for each other. Hey, let me in, will you? It's cold out here and I just need to talk. A lot has happened in the last couple of days and I need to know where you stand."

"Meet me at your car in two minutes."

Sam closed the door, and I handed her the gun.

"Get over the bridge and get the hell out of town now. I don't care who they are, anybody gets close to you, shoot them."

"Money, gas and I'm gone," she whispered. "Until next week."

We kissed and I watched her go into the garage.

Adler finished his cigarette and flipped the butt into the gutter as I came out. He smiled, but his face looked greasy and tired in the morning air. His suit had a cigarette burn on the right arm that looked fresh.

"How'd you find me?"

He shrugged. "Cop secrets, man. You know how it is."

I grabbed him by his coat collar. "How did you find me?"

"Traffic cameras, Johnny. You showed up at Kelly's house. Just ran a check. Do you think you're a sneaky guy? The broad's had the car ten years."

I let go of his jacket. He slumped forward.

"You're not on Kelly. What's your interest in him?"

"Johnny, my friend, I'm a cop. I'm interested in all kinds of crime. Inter-departmental help and all that."

We climbed into his car and I wanted to gag. The car stank of cigarettes and fast food. Wrappers lined the floor, and the windows were greasy yellow. An ashtray with a beanbag base sat on the console between the seats overflowing with half-finished cigarettes. Burns pocked the carpet and dash where he missed putting out his butts.

"Why are you here?" I asked.

"Just making sure you're safe like you been making sure my sister is safe. I'm watching your back."

"Good, then you can drive me someplace."

"I'm not your taxi."

"You're a public servant. Drive me downtown."

"Where?"

"To the police station."

Adler frowned, suspicion in his voice. "What you want there?"

"You going to threaten me, I want police protection."

"I haven't—you're twisting—"

"I can slap you around all day if I want, but I don't have the time, so think of yourself as the man of the hour. Everybody wants to hear what you have to say, especially my friends."

He looked like he would argue, maybe even put up a fight, but Roy Adler had given up fighting a long time ago. He knew it when he put the car into drive and pulled forward.

Once we were on the road, I asked, "Do you have a lighter?"

"Yeah."

"Know anything about what happened at Kelly's?"

"Go to hell, Johnny. I had nothing to do with that. Don't even try."

"Sure," I said and sat back watching the traffic.

About a mile from the station Adler pulled the car over and jammed the transmission into park. "We're not going downtown. We're going to talk."

"Works for me," I said, not moving.

"I'm a cop," he hissed. "And you're an ex-con. You torched Lou's place to get in good with Tancredi. You're afraid of the Russians and you know the cops can't help you.

You want to live, so you made a deal with Tancredi. He wanted Lou Kelly dead, so you did the deed for him. Only problem is now he knows you're wanted by the Russians so he's stepping out on you. That's where I come in. You need my help, but it will cost you. I want Tancredi."

"You thought all of that up on your own?" I asked. "I'm impressed, Roy. It's not accurate in any way, but I'm impressed you're looking at all the angles."

His voice was low. He sounded like a rat chittering in the hold of a cargo ship, his teeth all yellow and sharp. "You know who I work for, don't you?"

"I know. Always have. You came to visit me first, checking in on me. You're playing angles like everybody else, but the drugs got your brain scrambled and you're seeing things that don't exist, Roy."

"I could have you killed."

"By who? The Russians? Egorov is already coming for me. Once he's in country, the real fun begins."

His eyes widened, and I had to laugh.

"You're a transparent, bastard, I'll give you that. How stupid did you think I am, Roy? I thought it was Tancredi, at first. I got beat up at Lou's, and the boys went back to Tancredi and told him what happened. Them or him, somebody went to you as the man on the inside and once you got my description, you knew something wasn't right. You went right over to the motel. You had to. Only that wasn't it, was it? You were checking in for the Russians. You got the feeling I wasn't going anywhere, so you gave them the all clear sign and they left me alone."

"You're a twisted bastard, Johnny. You're the one with the funny ideas. You got some twisted angles in that brain of yours."

"I'm figuring out who I like and who I don't like, and right now you're not on my Christmas list."

"That's not funny. You should respect me more."

"Do you know where Tancredi is or do I have to hit your head against the steering wheel?"

Adler shook his head. "Nobody can find him. He moves around. We've tried for years to track him but he's paranoid, knows more about surveillance than we do. Doesn't stay at a place more than a day except for places like Charlie's. He stays there occasionally, but he knows we bug it, so nothing ever happens."

"How do I find him?"

"You don't, he finds you."

"Somebody has to know."

"Maybe your task force can help you. They've got more resources than I do. Understand, Johnny, you're trouble. I couldn't help you much even if I wanted. You walked in to a bar and beat two guys to pulp. You're making all kinds of people upset. There has to be some kind of justice."

I sat and laughed at him. He knew as much about justice as I knew about raising kittens. Even back when we were kids, he didn't know right from wrong and he's the one ended up a cop.

"What's so funny?"

"You talking about justice."

He gave me a sour look and changed the subject. "Charlie called me this morning. Said she went to see you the other night and told you the same thing I did. You should have listened."

"I heard her, I just didn't do what she wanted with what she told me."

"Don't you get *he's coming*? We got word this morning. You got maybe twenty-four hours! He's bringing guns, Johnny, like this city has never seen. Cops don't stand a chance.

Nobody does. Damn it, man, get out of here! Take my sister and go!"

"Your *sister?*" I stared at him incredulous. Then I thought about it from his perspective. Whatever they had done, they still cared about each other. Adler thought I could save his sister. He thought I could take her away and keep her safe. He had a brother's love so he didn't understand, nobody could keep her safe.

"I'll see you, Roy."

I climbed out of the car.

"I thought you wanted me to talk to somebody?"

"They wouldn't believe you anyway."

Adler swore at me as he raced the car away.

TWENTY-SIX

I walked to the police station and asked for Munroe. The sergeant behind the counter made a call, asked for him and listened. She hung up and said he left late last night. More questions would gain nothing so I asked her for a taxi and she pointed at a scratched and battered phone on the wall behind me.

After calling the cab company, I waited under the deep blue sky enjoying another day of being free and breathing. I soaked in both. When the cab arrived, I gave the driver the name of Julian's hospital and he hit the accelerator pushing me into the seat.

Fifteen minutes later I stood again in hospital registration giving the lady behind the counter Julian's name and asking to see him. She directed me to a new room on a new floor. I took the elevator up and found him sitting in a wheelchair, a pile of clothes and books in his lap and Ashley making one last check of the room.

"Johnny!" he said, as if we'd just had breakfast together this morning.

"I expected to find you still in bed enjoying the best the pharmacy had to offer."

He grinned. "No way. They're letting me out today. The earlier the better, I say."

Ashley said, "We're packed. We can leave now."

Julian smiled at her. "Give us a minute, please?"

The look she gave me said she didn't want to, but she stepped outside the room with huffy breath.

Julian wore bandages across his left arm, and a wide strip of gauze across the top of his head. Seeing him now moving around so freely, I realized it'd been five days since I'd visited and had wondered if he would make it. Five days felt like forever ago.

I thought of the men who put him in here and felt better. They wouldn't be leaving the hospital after five days; fifteen maybe.

Julian smiled and said, "Did I help?"

"You helped."

He grinned. "Guess it worked out."

I frowned. "Kelly's shop burned to the ground. The police found a body inside and suspect it's his."

"That's not possible," he said, but tears filled his eyes. "Lou is careful. He has fire alarms. He wouldn't do that."

"I think it's true."

"They're not sure, right?"

"Not yet."

He nodded. "Good. It's not him, not yet. Lou is good people." He didn't hold back or hide the tears falling down his cheeks. When he'd finished, while wiping his face with his sleeve, he said, "I'm not sure I'm crying for him or me or a little of both."

He searched my face, I didn't speak, but I understood. I didn't want to cry, I wanted to hurt someone.

He grabbed the handles of his wheelchair. "Now, I have to go. Ash and I are moving south, heading towards better weather. My legs, they're hurting, the cold isn't good for them." He pushed himself next to me and put his hand on my arm. "I won't come back, not ever. I can't. I'll find work somewhere else, someplace far from here. Lou taught me every man needs a purpose, something he can see in the mirror that makes himself proud. Do you have anything like that?"

"I do."

"Is it killing Tancredi?"

I shook my head. "Afterwards. I have something afterwards."

"Find me when this is over. I'd like to meet her."

I smiled.

He rolled to the door and spun the wheelchair around to face me. He'd had practice in the last five days. "Where's Lou's dog?"

"Dog?"

"His dog. Where is it?"

"I saw bowls at his place, but the dog wasn't there. I don't think he had time to board it."

Julian shook his head. "If Tancredi's men had seen him, wouldn't they would have shot him? Every time Tancredi came around the shop, the dog went nuts. Tancredi would have loved to shoot him."

"If he boarded the dog, he knew someone was coming."

"And that meant he didn't care to stop them."

"There wasn't a fight at the house. Kelly owns a shotgun, and he didn't fire it in the house. No blood, no guns, no dog."

"Maybe he gave up. Maybe he wanted to end it like this."

I remembered the way Kelly talked about the cancer. Would one way be easier to take than the other? Burning alive over being eaten alive by a disease? "If they took him, he didn't stop them. I woke the neighbors banging on the door. If they had heard gunshots, they would have called the police. He knew that."

"Find the dog," Julian said.

We shook hands and Ashley appeared. Positioning herself behind Julian's wheelchair, without a backwards glance, she pushed him to the elevator. I waited in the room to give them time to leave. All the electronic monitors were silently waiting for the next patient.

A line of taxis waited in front of the hospital. I climbed into the first one and gave him my destination. Finding waiting cabs surprised me so I mentioned it to the driver. He explained that during the day many people came and many people left, making for good business, so the drivers waited. I thought of the empty recovery room with its monitors and wondered about the poor bastard who would get it next. Would he arrive in a taxi, or maybe an ambulance? Would he even make it during his stay or would his last trip be into the hospital? I pushed the thoughts from my mind.

The cabbie drove me to Harker's office in silence: no radio, no conversation, no backward glances at me. He did his job and I did mine. I paid him, tipped him and climbed out like a good customer should. Fat snowflakes fell from the sky as he drove away. I climbed to the second floor of the plain two story building.

I knocked on the door and when nobody answered, I found it was unlocked. I let myself in. There was no sense being cold.

Rows of empty desks sat in the dark and I wondered at Harker's optimism. Had she expected the desks to be filled with aggressive cops hunting bad guys on the mean streets? From there, had she planned to oversee raids and night operations coordinated with State and Federal agencies? If so, this place was far from fulfilling her dream.

Harker appeared from a back office. She wore black slacks and a black turtleneck and held a white ceramic mug in her left hand. Wisps of steam floated up from the cup. "What are you doing here, Brogan?"

"Figuring out the next step."

"There is no next step. The operation shut down five hours ago. My bosses used your fight with Tancredi as an excuse to pull the plug. They claim the attention on Tancredi will make him go underground."

She waved me into her office with her coffee cup. I followed. She sat at the desk while I stood in the doorway. A lamp created an oval of light on her desk and a laptop turned the right side of her face blue.

"I'm sorry," I said.

"It was all bullshit. They never wanted us to find Egorov. We didn't get the manpower or the resources we needed. No boots on the ground means no intel and nothing to hit him with even if we found him."

Long tables ran along two sides of the office. Reams of printed paper sat on the tables slapped together with blue covers stamped with official seals. Several that looked like transcripts lay open on the table among scattered photos.

I walked over, picked one up. It was a good shot of me hitting the guy outside Sam's diner. I showed it to Harker. "You or Munroe?"

"Him."

"He wondered if you ever slept. Did either of you?"

"One of the many reasons I like working with him."

I put the photo down and asked, "Where's Tancredi?"

"Do you think this is a playground with schoolyard rules? Two bullies duke it out while everyone else stands around cheering them on? People are getting hurt, killed, and the rest of us are losing careers and families."

"I need your help finding him."

"We don't know where he is."

"I think you have an idea, a list, something. You're a smart cop and you're just as angry about this as I am."

She shook her head. "I'm not going to authorize my last asset to go on a killing spree over an old cancer riddled man he barely knew."

I hung my head as I rubbed my eyes with my fingers.

"I'm sorry. I shouldn't have said that. Munroe spoke highly of him."

"Where is Munroe?"

"He won't help you. This was a career case, supposed to get us into command so we could make an actual difference. You blew that."

"Munroe was with me when I saw Kelly last. We tried to convince Kelly to get out but he refused."

"Munroe was with you?"

"Yes. Why?"

"He never mentioned it in his status reports."

"So? Maybe he hasn't filled them out yet. What cop likes paperwork?"

"I haven't seen him all weekend."

"I talked with him Saturday and Sunday."

"Where?"

"Over the phone. I called the station, got his desk."

She shook her head. "We forward calls. You'd never know if you were talking to him at his desk or the beach."

"So where the hell is he?"

Harker picked up her phone and called Munroe. In the silence, I could hear the phone ringing. There was no answer. A click and a metallic version of his voice said to leave a message. Harker put the phone down. "He might be at home."

"Get me Tancredi's location," I said.

She reached for the cup of coffee, her hand shaking under the desk light. She noticed and pulled it out of the light. "It's over. There's nothing left to do."

"Get me Tancredi's location."

She hung her head forward and rubbed her neck. The stress bunched her muscles so tight I could see them. She took deep breaths and sat up. "The ruse to get you out of prison was solid—it had to be to convince Egorov—so you're free to go. I would suggest getting out of the state."

"When is Egorov arriving?"

She took another deep breath and let it out. "I think he's here now. We have audio up in several locations and over the last two days the conversations have changed. They're moving now, not waiting." She pointed at the blue books. "I've been reviewing the transcripts and I think he's here now running the business."

Son of a bitch. I had less time than I thought.

"Where do you have the bugs?"

"I can't give you details about an ongoing police investigation."

"You said the operation shut down five hours ago. Why don't you give me a history lesson?"

Another deep breath. "There are—were—three locations. One is a dock where they bring in most of the drugs. The second is an office downtown, but they haven't used it the last two weeks because they can't protect it as well as the other locations. The last place is the Russia House. Most of the men are staying there and it's where we expected Egorov to go once he arrived. They move it around every couple of weeks, but they stay in the same neighborhood, most of which they own."

"The Russia House?"

"Their main base of operations. We set up audio across the street in an abandoned house. Last year we got a man inside, but they killed him and left him outside the station with fourteen broken bones. After that, we couldn't get volunteers."

"Can you enter the house with overwhelming force and arrest everyone?"

"If we had documented evidence, I could push it through. Could even do it under the radar and justify myself afterwards. But right now, the audio is clean. They have someone in the department."

I walked to the window and searched for the river. The sun had set, and though the snowfall obscured the view, I knew it was out there to the east. "How do you change the soul of a city?"

"You can't," Harker said. "You can't change people. Once they rot, they can't return. Like the honest person who tells a terrible lie. After that, there's always doubt."

I found the bridge and watched cars drive across, their headlights making the snow sparkle.

"It's the wrong goal," I said. "You can't change a city. You can't change those who don't want to change. Men like Tancredi and Egorov are the big lie but it goes much deeper. Every person who sanctions their actions, whether through fear or indifference, is helping them spread it. We can't stop those people. They either won't learn or don't care to."

"What's your point?"

"The only thing you can do is live. There are injustices in the world, there are evil men, there are cheap politicians, there are corrupt cops. They will make your job harder and you may never live in a city where justice exists, but you have to do the best you can."

Harker walked around her desk and stood next to me. "It's bullshit, but I'd vote for you on that platform."

"I wouldn't make a good politician. Don't care for manipulating people's lives."

She smiled. "I don't have Tancredi's location, but he has two women he sees regularly. He moves them routinely, but they're easy to keep tabs on. I'll get you what I have."

I watched the snow fall while she dug around in the reams of paper. She handed me a single typed page. Charlie's name was easy enough to find. The address didn't look like the place I'd visited so that meant she'd moved again. "Have you and Munroe checked these places?"

"Yes."

"Are you giving me the list because you don't think I'll find anything?"

Harker shrugged. "Who knows, maybe you're a better cop than we are." She put her coat on. "Can I drop you somewhere?"

"Why are you being nice now?"

"I played by the rules because they were the right rules. My partner is missing, the brass sold me out and the public doesn't care. Now you're going to bust my balls for being nice to a wrongly imprisoned citizen?"

I called a cab from her office phone and afterwards followed her down the stairs. She stopped under the awning and said, "I have no answers, Brogan. Whatever you do, it's on you."

Flakes of snow the size of quarters landed on her hair as she walked through the parking lot to her car. I watched her brush off the windshield, climb in and drive away, the tires slipping into the ruts made by other vehicles.

My coat wasn't heavy enough for the weather, but I had a

cap and gloves so I leaned against the building with my hands pressed as deep into the coat as I could get them and watched the street fill with snow again.

TWENTY-SEVEN

I waited under the awning for the taxi to arrive when a car came speeding around the corner. The driver expertly navigated the large black automobile across the road as if the snow didn't exist. The car plowed through the parking lot and stopped ten feet away, its headlights pinning me.

Casual, methodical and with no unnecessary motions to draw attention to himself, the driver stepped out and pointed a short-barreled rifle in my direction.

The passenger slipped out of the car slower, but still with a practiced air. Weighing over two hundred pounds and wearing a heavy black coat, he moved efficiently across the ice in six steps and stopped in front of me with empty hands. He glanced left, right and said, "You come with us."

He didn't say, "You come with me" or "The boss wants to see you", but "You come with us." He had friends, not just him and the driver, but him, the driver and guys I wouldn't see unless I became problematic.

I raised my arms and he patted me down—not rough, not unpleasant, just a professional doing a routine job. He stepped to the back-passenger door and opened it. I stepped inside and sat on expensive leather. He closed the door and climbed into the passenger seat. The driver backed the car, quiet and smooth, over the snow and out of the lot.

A man sat next to me with a gun resting in his lap with the barrel pointed toward my gut. He made the gun look like an afterthought, as if he held a cigarette. Medium build, dark hair, wearing a quality, discreet suit like a magazine model of a Russian businessman. Even white teeth appeared in a practiced smile.

"Took you long enough," I said.

A glass plate divided the front and back of the car. No one responded. I swore under my breath. I was on my own. Nobody would look for me when I went missing. Harker was off the case, Munroe was in the wind and Adler was as good as a cup of sand in the Sahara. Julian was leaving town and Sam was gone. She would come back in two weeks. And besides, what could she do? In two weeks, I'd be thirteen days dead. She could file a police report, I guess.

"You Petr?" I asked.

I knew he wasn't Egorov. He looked nothing like Egorov had in the picture Munroe showed me. But people want to answer questions. There's a symmetry to it: one asks, one answers. We do it so often, we itch when no answer is forthcoming.

"No," he said.

I felt relief. I had broken him. At least that's what I told myself while I sat on expensive leather smelling bourbon and looking at the muzzle of a gun.

"Good. Petr wouldn't need to point a gun at me."

He smiled. His teeth were not just white, but unnaturally white as if he'd used a chemical to strip them of any color. The gun didn't waver. He was accustomed to this kind of talk. He probably liked it.

"Why wait so long to pick me up?"

"Petr wants to keep an eye on you. He's concerned."

"Tancredi," I said.

"Yes, Tancredi. You upset him. We're concerned he might try something rash. Petr doesn't like rash."

"You weren't concerned before?"

"The rules prevented you from having a gun. We calculated you would beat people up but that was all. You are good at beating people up and you are not rash."

"What happens now?"

"We keep you safe until Petr arrives."

"Safe so Petr can kill me?"

He said nothing.

"I have a few things I need to do first," I said. "Tancredi is one of them."

"Don't worry about Tancredi. We solve problems. As you say, *good customer service.*"

"I'm a hands-on kind of guy. I like taking care of my own problems. I would hate to owe Petr a favor."

"We'll take care of it."

I knew I had to get out of the car. Being here wouldn't get me what I needed. I had too much to do still. As happy as I was knowing where the Russians were, I wanted to take care of Tancredi myself. I owed him for Kelly.

The snow thickened and the driver turned on the wipers. The passenger said something and the driver snapped a response. He turned the wipers on faster, but they only smeared the heavy flakes into long strips of ice across the windshield. Visibility decreased and the passenger cursed in English. He grunted a comment the driver ignored while lowering his window and reaching out to grab the blade. He got it on the third try and slapped it, spilling white slush across the window and himself. He fell back into his seat rolling up the window.

The air was bitter in the back of the car even with the divider. The streetlights flashed past a fuzzy yellow, and the intersection lights cut through the snow as dots of flashing red. All of it was three shades darker through the tinted windows. The city was shutting down.

I turned back to the man with the gun. "How much further?" I asked. "I want a shower and food."

His eyes narrowed and the gun tightened in his hand. He glanced towards the front of the car, then back at me. He said nothing.

That was good for him, bad for me. A professional, he wouldn't acknowledge my ribbing. I pointed at the driver. "Hey, you're driving too fast. Don't you people have snow in Russia?"

It had the effect I wanted. The driver glanced in the mirror. A wiry guy, he shouldn't have been driving; he was too jumpy, too easy to distract. The passenger said something and the driver glanced at him, not at the road. The guy next to me spoke up, "Ignore him."

He moved the gun butt up to use it as a club to hit me. I lunged forward, grabbing his wrist and the gun. His eyes widened but he didn't speak.

I twisted the gun towards the roof, jammed my finger in the trigger guard and squeezed. The gun went off flashing in the dark space. The bullet tore into the roof and the smell of burnt powder filled the space.

The blast startled the driver who panicked and swerved the car to the right and left while trying to see us in the rearview mirror. The front seat passenger yelled. We hit a parked car slamming everyone forward. No one wore seat belts. The driver hit the windshield and sprayed blood on the glass. He fell back to his seat and slumped to one side. The passenger hit the windshield and bounced back into his seat. He didn't have the added damage from a steering wheel to knock him out, but he sat stunned. I didn't have long. The man next to me responded faster than I expected but not fast enough.

We twisted and tumbled around in the seat. I crushed his hand under the gun and it went off again, this time the bullet hit the bulletproof side window. It ricocheted and buried itself in the roof. I was deaf and disorientated but I was on top.

He hugged his arms in and angled the gun at my face and damn near blew it off with the third squeeze of the trigger. The bullet went over my head, but the flash blinded and the blast stung my face. I jammed my knees on his chest, twisted the gun in his hand and raked my elbow across his face. He went limp. I untangled the gun from his hand and shot him in the chest.

The driver stirred and the passenger fumbled with the glove compartment. I shot him in the head and then the driver.

The street was empty. In both directions, as far as I could see, the intersection lights blinked red. Commercial buildings rose into the snowy darkness overhead. It came down so hard the windshield was covered by the time I had searched the corpses finding a hat, gloves and scarf. I considered taking the guns, but I didn't like being on the street with them.

I got out of the car, stepped into a foot of snow and walked to the nearest corner to orientate myself, then walked west on empty streets.

Walking across town reminded me of my first night out of prison, but this time I had better shoes and clothes. What I didn't have was any idea how long it would take to get back to Sam's. I didn't know my exact location, and my best estimate was one hour on foot under the current conditions.

I didn't try running. One slip and I could easily hit the ice and knock myself out. Instead, I walked in the middle of the street until I heard a street plow coming up the next block. Bright blue lights flashed off the snow, the driver a shapeless thing in a dark aquarium tank. The orange hulk cut through the snow and cleared me a path which quickened my pace.

The sky was light gray when I walked up to Sam's front door. Its porch light was out and the street was empty except for eighteen inches of snow. Around back, I found nothing parked in the alley on that block or the next. Only one house had snow cleared and only to the end of the driveway.

The spare key was under a snow-covered rock near the back door, but I didn't need it because one of the window panes was busted out of the backdoor. I hesitated, listening, but no sounds came from inside. I stood there wishing I had taken a gun.

I walked in and turned on the light over the stove. The place was trashed worse than Kelly's. The method was the same purposeful destruction. The veins in my neck throbbed and my mouth went dry. I wanted to hurt whoever had done this to Sam's house. There's a fragility in a woman's home, a feeling I didn't get at Kelly's, that hit me now seeing the place so utterly wrecked. Clean towels tossed to the floor and covered in muddy snow, a picture of a blue flower in a vase cut with a knife and tossed in the sink, her books scattered across the floor, their pages twisted and bent never to be straight again. Pictures were cut from their frames, the faces disfigured. Everything was overturned in the bedroom. I grabbed the mattress, flattened it out, fell on it and went to sleep.

When I woke up I wished I hadn't. I tried for thirty

minutes to go back to sleep, but the pain was too much. I stumbled into the bathroom and found pills, swallowed them dry and went back to the mattress. When I woke again it was dark outside. My body no longer hurt but I needed to eat badly.

Stumbling into the kitchen I dug through the cupboards, the refrigerator and the freezer. I found two pork chops and a bucket of flower so I cooked the pork chops frozen and dumped flower on them. I stood there the entire time they cooked thinking I could eat them half raw. I ate them hot and burned myself, and mopped up the grease from the pan with a slice of stale bread.

I went back to the mattress and slept.

When I woke next, I stripped off my clothes, took more pain pills—half as many this time—and showered. It was a slow painful process but the pills kicked in making it easier. When I had finished, I used a towel to dry off and dug around in the piles of clothes on the floor until I found a set of mine Sam had left behind.

Clean and dressed, I checked the bruises in the mirror. They wouldn't win me any contests, but neither would they draw any unwanted attention.

I found the spare roll of money I'd hidden at the top of Sam's closet and counted it out. I had enough to do what needed to be done today. But first I needed to eat again. I walked to the diner where Sam used to work and sat at the same booth I'd sat in last week. This time it wasn't Sam but the lady who had given me the stink eye the night we met.

She gave me the stink eye again and said, "She quit and left town."

"Good," I said. "Steak and eggs, please."

"She said you were a good guy. Said you treated her well, took care of her car. So why did she leave?"

"You should stop talking about her if you want to keep her safe."

She frowned. "I hate this town."

She left and returned with a coffee pot and cup. I finished three cups before she returned with the steak. She set it in front of me and asked, "Will she be OK?"

"Yes," I said.

It was the best answer I could give her, but it didn't feel like enough.

TWENTY-EIGHT

I took a taxi from the diner to Kelly's house, paid the driver and walked inside. I tried one more time to find the shotgun, but found the keys to Kelly's truck instead. Locking the house behind me, I climbed into the truck, backed it out to the driveway and let the engine warm while I reviewed Harker's list of Tancredi's possible locations. Charlie's name was third from the bottom. I memorized the address and put the truck in gear.

The address took me to a six-story apartment building that was different from the bird cage Tancredi used for Charlie and the other girls. A buzzer on a locked door made up the building security so I jammed buttons on the intercom until somebody let me in. Charlie's unit was on the top floor at the far corner. I figured the place had a decent view of the river, but it wasn't exactly as she described the last time we spoke.

I stood to one side and knocked on the door. It opened fast like someone had been standing behind it waiting.

Tancredi appeared and pushed a gun into my chest. He said, "Get in here."

I put my hands up so he could see them and strolled into the room.

"Where is she?" he asked. "Where's Charlie?"

"I'm looking for you."

"How'd you know I'd be here?"

"I stole a list of names from the cops. Been hunting you all morning," I lied.

His eyebrows squished together while he considered what I said.

I didn't want him deciding it would be easier to shoot me so I continued, "The cops quit the case against you because they're trying to get Egorov. I figure you and I work something out, because we both want the same thing."

"Yeah, what's that?"

"Egorov dead."

He smiled. "Word is he's after you." He shook his head. "You had your chance to play nice, but I've got a different plan now. Stand over there, I need to frisk you."

I let him frisk me, and when he was done, he pointed at a chair where I made myself comfortable. He sat across from me with the gun pointed at my chest.

"You worried about the gun?"

"With your finger on the trigger and your adrenalin through the roof, yes. You hear the wrong thing, you panic and pull the trigger. You're not a careful man so I wouldn't be surprised if you shot me unintentionally."

"Maybe I'll do it intentionally."

"You won't. You made a mistake with the Russians and I'm your peace offering."

He gave me a nasty grin. "You got it worked out, right? So damn smart. I might just shoot you to make a point. I don't give a damn about the Russians. I've been working their territories for months now. They're bleeding. The only reason Egorov is coming is because I've been putting pressure on his men. I don't want a turf war but I want them out. You're my way of getting a face to face with Petr so I can end this."

"Call them. Petr should be here today. You have a way of contacting them I assume. Call them, please."

Tancredi smiled. "You're a tough son of a bitch, I'll give you that. But we're not doing that yet. We're waiting on the woman to get back."

The apartment was good sized. The huge window I expected to look upon the river wasn't as big as I imagined but it was still large. I could see ice and snow covering the world, and the occasional steam and exhaust rising from houses and cars. The room was laid out tastefully. Tancredi was on the couch and I was in a chair. A couple more chairs sat around a giant glass coffee table in the center of the room. On the table was an oversized book about fashion. A liquor cabinet sat in one corner.

"How many rooms in this place?" I asked

"You thinking about renting here?"

"Making sure you checked the place."

"I've been here since yesterday. I checked the place."

"Why are you waiting on this woman? What'd she do?"

"I want something she stole from me."

"You think maybe she's gone, split town?"

"No, she's got loyalty."

"She stole from you."

He shrugged. "She'll be here."

He went to the liquor cabinet. I was ten feet away and he could see me in the mirror over the cabinet. I wouldn't get to him by the time he shot me. He knew it so he set the gun on the cabinet and made himself a drink. I didn't ask for one.

"I'm surprised you let me live," I said.

Tancredi smiled. He liked me talking about him. "I admit I had other plans. Turns out I'm not so good at real estate like I'd hoped, and it is true my backers are not happy, but by giving you to the Russians instead of killing you myself, I can get two things accomplished. You dead and my backers reimbursed. Everyone is happy."

"I won't be happy."

He shrugged.

"You think they'll let you live?"

"Mind games don't work with me. They made a deal, they'll keep their end."

"Like you?"

He picked up the gun and walked back to his seat with the drink. He took a sip and sneered at me. "They were right. You are a bastard. But yes, they'll keep their word. You've pissed them off good."

I shrugged. "Why'd you kill, Lou?"

Tancredi considered, then raised his glass in a toast. "To old friends and adversaries."

"Why'd you kill him? You didn't need to do that."

He smiled at me sadly. "He burned himself up in that shop of his. Was unsafe to begin with. Fire codes and all that. He should have taken better care of his property. I didn't kill him, Brogan, I had no reason to. I had the law on my side. It was a matter of time before I had the place. Oh, I knew about the legal tricks he played, but those were child's games compared to what my lawyers can do. I would have had that property within the week. So now my plans change. I have to work with the Russians instead of competing with them."

"You're lying."

He shook his head. "You're stubborn also."

A key rattled in the door. Tancredi set his glass down and sprang to one side so he could see me and the door. He was faster than I had expected him to be. I didn't move.

"Get in here," Tancredi said, pointing the gun at Charlie.

She walked into the room carrying a half dozen shopping bags. "What's going—Why are you pointing that gun at me?"

"Drop those bags."

She looked at the floor, shrugged and let them drop to the carpet.

Tancredi's eyes narrowed. "What's in those bags?"

When Charlie didn't answer, Tancredi kicked one over with his foot. Children's clothes spilled onto the floor. "What's this?"

"I went shopping."

"For children's clothes? What the hell? You told me you can't get pregnant. What the hell is this about?"

"Remember I told you about my pregnant friend, Janet? I spent the night with her and thought she'd like the surprise of some new clothes."

"Hello," I said.

Charlie turned, saw me and the color drained from her cheeks, but it was hard to notice through the makeup. She turned back to Tancredi. "What's going on here?" she asked.

"I've got business with this man."

"And it involves *guns*? Why are you pointing a gun at *me*?"

Tancredi was fast. He hit her across the face with his open palm but she didn't cry out. Charlie wasn't that kind of woman. "Don't," he said. "Don't you play games with me, woman. I want my money back."

"I don't—"

He brought his hand up again. "Don't lie, Charlie. Your games are cute, but not when they involve ripping me off. Where is it?"

"Where's—"

He slapped her again, this time she groaned quietly. No anger in the sound just acceptance.

"Charlie," he said. "You might make it out of this alive if you stop lying to me."

"I'm sorry. I have it. It's not here but I can get it."

Tancredi nodded. "Good, that's good. Now go make dinner."

"You...you want dinner right now?"

"I have you. The money's not going anywhere without you. And I'm hungry. Make chicken or something."

"Chicken?" She asked, looking at me.

I looked between the two of them. Now I understood. They deserved each other.

Charlie reached her hand to her face but didn't touch it. The heavy makeup was smeared now and the swelling had started.

"I would like a drink first," she said. She moved to the liquor cabinet and picked up a decanter. Then looked at me. "Would you like one Mister—"

"Brogan," I said.

"Well, Mister Brogan, would you like something to drink? I can see *he* didn't offer you one."

"Scotch neat."

Tancredi didn't protest but sat down on the couch and sipped his own. The gun he set on the arm rest. Charlie glanced at it and then at him. His eyes were heavy but he stared back at her.

When she'd finished making the drinks, she handed me mine and went into the kitchen. I took a gulp letting it warm my insides.

Tancredi picked up the phone next to him and made a call. "Yes," he said, "I have the guy you're looking for. Brogan. Right." Tancredi gave him the address and hung up the phone. "You got your wish. We have about thirty minutes."

Several minutes passed as Charlie dinged pots and pans, opened and closed the refrigerator and chopped vegetables on a cutting board. She emerged from the kitchen flushed, carrying a tray she brought to me tilted away from Tancredi. Crackers lined the edges, different colored cheeses lay in a circle around the outer edge and in the center was the gun she'd pointed at me last week.

"Cracker?" she asked.

I considered those big beautiful eyes and wondered what went on behind them. I realized, for the first time, I truly didn't know. I imagined black smoke hid dark corners in terrible haunted spaces I could never visit. I shivered.

"Guests first," she said.

It was a hell of a play. I pick up the gun, she steps to one side and I blow a hole in Tancredi. He stares stupidly at me and falls over dead. In Charlie's world, life was that simple.

Doing it herself wasn't her style. She set it up for me, made everything easy, but I had to sweat through the heavy lifting.

Then I thought of Kelly and it became easy.

I took the gun. It felt heavy and powerful in my hand. I assumed she chambered a cartridge, because if she didn't we'd both be dead. She stepped to one side.

Tancredi's eyes opened wide—his drink halfway to his mouth, the gun too far away on the arm rest. I shot him. The bullet tore into his chest, the glass fell to the floor, his gun remained motionless. I thought about what Lou said of the rot and those responsible. Maybe Killing Tancredi didn't matter, not in the big picture, but it mattered to me. I shot him again, and he slumped forward dead.

Charlie placed the tray on the table and flung herself into

my lap. I held the gun, and I held her, and I wondered bitterly what made them different.

"We make a hell of a team, Johnny. You didn't hesitate."

"You should have shot him. You had reason enough."

"Don't be petulant. You did well. I'm proud of you."

"Making you proud has never brought me joy."

"Johnny, defending my honor is your job. You know why? You're my knight. You'll always come back to me. You'll always save me."

"Do you remember what I said last week?"

She kissed my cheek. "Last week doesn't matter. Only today matters. Why do you need to be so critical? Look how far we've come. You killed a man to save me. That's love."

"I don't love you, Charlie. I don't think I ever did."

"You're just saying that."

I pushed her off my lap and she fell to the floor. Her bottom lip quivering, she reached out and held onto my leg.

"You don't mean that, Johnny. Your head's just spinning because you shot a man. It can mess you up for a while but you'll get over it. You'll feel better soon and you'll realize you shouldn't have said what you're saying. You'll remember I helped save your life."

"Charlie, you should have left him a long time ago."

She stood, went to the liquor cabinet and picked up a pack of cigarettes. I looked at the wet mess that had been Tancredi. She shook one of the cigarettes loose and pushed it into her mouth. The lighter bobbed, chasing the tip and missing several times before she had it lit. She stared at me through the smoke, those eyes smoldering as hot as the cigarette's cherry.

"I need your brother's address," I said.

"Of course, you do. You always need something from me. You give me nothing, but you take everything."

"He's the next link. I need him to find the Russians."

"Are you trying to find the Russia House?"

"Do you know where it is?"

"They move around a lot. I thought Tancredi was paranoid, he's nothing compared to them."

"Do you know where they are?"

"No."

"Does your brother?"

"Why not wait for the men coming here?"

"Someone heard the gunfire and called the cops. I'm not sure if they or the Russians will be here first and I don't have the time or energy to have a cop walk in on me torturing a guy."

"Would you beat it out of my brother?"

"I'll ask politely."

"But not too politely, right?"

She read in my silence what she wanted and seemed to come away satisfied because she found a pad of paper and wrote his address. When she handed it to me she asked, "Did it bother you killing him?" She indicated Tancredi. "Were you afraid?"

"No," I said, putting the paper and her gun in my coat pocket. I retrieved Tancredi's keys from his pocket and started towards the door. "You need to leave."

Tears filled her eyes as she looked at me in the mirror. "I won't be here when you get back."

"Charlie, I won't be back."

She flung the lighter at me but it missed, hit the wall instead. Then she ran at me and brought her open hand up. I caught it and she stumbled, fell to her knees and cried. She reached out and touched my leg. "I love you, Johnny. Damn it, I love you. Can't you see that? We were meant to be together."

I was at the door when she cried, "I won't be here when you get back! I won't, damn you! I'm gone. Gone forever!"

TWENTY-NINE

I tossed Tancredi's keys into a trashcan on the way out of the building and then spent an hour driving Kelly's truck to Adler's house because snow buried most of the streets. Two blocks from his house I gave up trying to get through and parked the truck on a street which hadn't seen a plow since this morning. Most of the sidewalk was clear, though Adler's strip contained a foot of snow. Neighbors on either side had pushed into his section a few feet, enough to show how neighborly they were. The strip contained no footprints, not even the mailman's.

I walked to the front door and rang the bell. When no one answered, I tried again. I stepped back and walked around the house looking in the windows. Heavy white curtains blocked the view into the living room. The next window had clear plastic sheets taped over it for insulation. A bedroom probably. Good for someone who sleeps all kinds of hours like a cop or a junkie.

A wooden slatted fence blocked side access to the house. There were no tracks on the ground which meant a dog wasn't likely. I jumped the fence and made my way to the back door where I found two distinct sets of tracks. They moved through the garage, towards the house and then away. They walked over the yard to a patio attached to the house. The patio was indistinct under all the snow, but the railings were visible. I tried the door and it moved easily on its track letting snow tumble in onto a tile floor. I stepped into the kitchen, felt Charlie's gun in my coat pocket, but left it there knowing I wouldn't need it.

I was right. I walked into the living room and found Adler strapped with thin wire to a kitchen chair, blood oozing from cuts where the wire dug into his naked body. Dried blood crusted his ankles and the dining room floor. Long gashes ran along his arms and legs exposing the muscle and fat. A gun taped to his right hand sat in his lap. He turned his head towards me, staring in my direction through a blood filled right eye. Both of his lips were missing, exposing bent teeth.

A woman and a teenage girl sat across from him on a couch. Both were naked and both were dead. The ring finger of the woman's left hand rested on the coffee table, a silver ring still on it.

Adler giggled at me and made words, mangled and barely audible. Blood and saliva oozed out of his mouth as he spoke. "Hell ov a harty, hohnny. You sooda cone. They ass about you."

I walked into the dining room. "Where are they?"

He stared at his wife's ring finger on the table. "One cartridge. Shooting you would redeen me, they said. They'd take ne 'ack." He groaned a wild desperate sound. "They cut my liths off. Who cones 'ack fron that?"

"Where are they?"

His head fell to the side, and he looked up at me with his one good eye. "Twell hours. I've 'een here twell hours. I juss wanna get high. Once, juss once. I wann to get high so 'ad."

"Tell me where they are."

His face contorted and I realized it would have been a smile if he could have smiled. "Can't e'en lih my hand. Wann to kill mysell. Three hours. Too weak."

I said nothing.

"Crawl sace in the masser 'edroom. E'ery dine I e'er stole. Take it…Send on e'ery gun you can 'uy. Use it again' those bas'ards." He laughed then. "We'll get 'en. We'll get 'en good."

He faded, his one good eye dull, staring up at the ceiling.

"Where are they, Roy?"

He told me.

I lifted the gun, pointed it at his head and he pulled the trigger.

THIRTY

I drove the truck within the speed limit. The roads were clear and traffic was light. I felt empty, almost light headed. My breathing came easy. I took my time driving through the Russian neighborhood. The truck bottomed out in potholes, most of the houses needed bulldozing and several cars sat gutted in yards. It was well after dark, and people hung out around burning dumpsters hugging brown paper bags to their chests. Much of the debris hid under gray snow, but piles of wood, cardboard and broken fences poked through.

Someone had driven over the green street sign and left the twisted metal uprooted in the street. I parked the truck next to it, turned off the lights and left the engine running. Snow plows had come through earlier in the evening, but the neighborhood didn't look like they paid enough taxes for a single pass. Someone had wanted the overtime.

The house was the third from the corner up the next block. Calling it the Russia House was a misnomer. With its steep gables, cracked balustrades, and dormers with blackened glass, it was about as Victorian as you could get and practically a fortress. It was as if the Victorians had planned for sniper rifles and machine guns. The houses on either side appeared abandoned, the windows dark and broken. A rickety metal fence wound around the yard like makeshift concertina wire.

I turned off the engine and stepped out of the truck. Snow crunched under my boots as I stepped over the berm created by a snowplow. Snow covered cars lined both sides of the street, their windows hidden, their tires buried. I had a block and a half to walk. I pulled up the collar on my coat and stuffed my hands into my pockets. This time I had a gun. One bullet in the chamber. Seven bullets in the magazine. It would have to be enough.

At the corner of the next block I stopped. Several plows had cleared this street. The berms were higher and even the sidewalks had seen a shovel. Curtains moved in the front window of a house on the left side of the street. The porch lights flickered once, twice and remained on. An old man wearing a snow suit, carrying a shovel moved to the end of his driveway where he paused readying himself for an hour of hard work. Simultaneously, we took deep breaths and I stepping forward as he sliced his blade into the snow.

I crossed the street and saw a car idling on my right. Munroe sat in the driver's seat. We saw each another, but neither moved. He put the car in drive and inched towards me. I stepped to the driver's window.

He lowered it and I smelled cold stale fast food. A wrapper sat on the seat next to him. He'd laid it out like a dinner tray: a burger, fries, and a pile of sticky mayonnaise on one corner like paint on an easel.

"Get back in Lou's truck and follow me."

I could hit him, maybe knock him out, but at this angle with a simple punch to his face I doubted it would happen.

He might call it in but more than likely he'd get out of his car and shoot me. I could argue with him, figure out a way to get out of this, except he wasn't debating me, he was telling me to follow him somewhere. It didn't feel like he was a cop trying to stop me, it felt like we were coconspirators. He knew something had happened to Tancredi.

"You going to stop me?" I asked.

"We need to talk."

I nodded, turned and walked back past the old man in the driveway. He'd made progress, but he wouldn't finish by the time the sun came up in the morning. Maybe he knew. Maybe he preferred it that way. He was pacing himself.

The truck was still warm. Munroe pulled to the next block, and I followed him. I stayed back about three car lengths. We didn't go far, maybe a mile. He pulled into a parking ramp, the kind used for parking to take a city bus. This one had six levels, all empty. A plow moved around the lot clearing space for non-existent cars.

Munroe drove to the second level, parking his car along the same side as the Russia House. I pulled up next to him, turned off the truck and climbed into his car. He had crumpled the wrapper and the bag and tossed it to the floor. He rolled his window down halfway, paused and rolled it back up.

"I'm quitting," he said, maybe to himself, maybe to me. "I want to live through this, you do too. You go in there without firepower and you'll get killed."

I felt the gun in my coat pocket. Cold steel and plastic, solid, accurate to maybe thirty yards if the target didn't move. A solid firearm, but it didn't increase my confidence in any way. If the men wore body armor, which was unlikely but possible, or if they had machine guns, I wouldn't stand a chance—not that I stood much of a chance. I tried thinking of a better way to end this but came up with nothing. Tonight would be up close and personal.

"Egorov was supposed to make my career," he continued. "I gave three years of my life for this case. They pulled it right out from under us. We were fools."

"Tancredi is dead."

He nodded. "Heard it on the radio. You're not too hard to follow, you know. Lou was my friend so that doesn't hurt my feelings any. Funny, everyone used the Russians for something: Harker and I wanted a career, Tancredi wanted prestige, you wanted a job. They didn't deliver on anybody's dreams. We all bet wrong."

"Why did you come?" I asked.

"We didn't stop Tancredi in time."

"We didn't."

"We're not great cops."

"I don't have a badge," I said.

"You have a gun. In this city that's all you need."

He picked up a new pack of gum, tore open the silver wrapper and shoved a piece in his mouth. He chewed on it a few times, swallowed it and laughed. "As a kid I was told gum stayed in your stomach for seven years. I didn't think about that until I quit smoking. I'm eating so much of it it's going to clog my guts up."

I waited.

"You do have Charlie's gun, right?"

"Yes."

"Did you kill Tancredi with it?"

Maybe Charlie got away, maybe she didn't. It was unlikely she would talk to the cops. Munroe came on his own. Alone, no backup, no visible intention of arresting me. I didn't answer.

"You need to trust someone, Brogan. You can't go in there

with just that gun. I've run surveillance on the Russians for a long time, and I've never seen them this well-armed and ready to kill. They know their fields of fire and they're careful. We've tried different avenues of approach, all the usual routines, and they jammed us up every time."

"What else?"

"Egorov is inside. There's too much activity for him not to be. The rest of the city is shut down with the storm, but it's like Defender of the Fatherland Day with all the activity inside that house. They're readying for something big. Part of that involves you I think. They're trying to find you and they will kill you and then they will find anyone else who might even remotely know you. That includes me, Harker and anyone else you might have smiled at once. You escaped them twice and you killed Tancredi. Egorov wants you dead."

"You're sure Egorov is in the house?"

"Are you listening? Yes, he's in there but you're not going to get him."

"Harker said the operation is over. They have no reason to come after you. Killing cops won't do them any good. It's too big of a spotlight."

"Killing cops in this town doesn't bring the spotlight it used to. They want the city running to their beat. Egorov started a war, the kind he can win."

"Why are you here?"

"He knows we went after him. Harker and I don't stand a chance now. That…that I can handle. But he won't stop there. He'll go after our families. He needs to be stopped."

"And you're here to help?"

"In a way. Everything you'll need is in the trunk."

"Why not just bring in police? They want him and you know where he is. You've got a case."

"We had an incomplete case, but we got shut down because of your play against Tancredi. A weak excuse for sure, but these people don't care about the truth. Its appearances that matter. Harker and I fooled ourselves into thinking we could get Egorov, but we never stood a chance. They manipulated us as much as you." He took a deep breath. "Egorov is in country. He should have been in prison eight hours ago."

"This why you're helping me?"

"Egorov was a career case, but not any longer, not to me. It's about a system that lets guys like that get away. We're doing that, we're letting the bad guys win, and we're crying about it like we can't do anything but go home and wait with our families to get murdered. But maybe, just maybe, one or two of us does something and things turn around."

"You going in there with me?"

He frowned. "No. I'll help, but not in that way. I can't. I've got a wife and kids I want to go home to."

"For how long?" I asked. "If I don't make it this time, if I don't kill Egorov, he's coming after you. He'll kill you, your family and everyone you ever cared about. You said it yourself."

"I'll help. I will. There's an empty house across the street. Been abandoned for months. We used it to get closer to the house. I'll set up a distraction in there to give you a chance at maybe surviving."

He stepped out of the car and said, "Come on, let's earn some trust."

I followed him to the back of the car. He popped the trunk open. Three high quality duffle bags filled the space. He opened first one, then the second, then the third. Inside each were several shotguns and pistols. In the third bag was a bulletproof vest.

"Should be enough guns for anything you need to do today. Pick what you want and when you're done with them, toss them in the river. Do the same with Charlie's gun."

"Ammo?"

"In the bag underneath."

I dug out the ammo bag, opened it and found twenty boxes of 9mm ammo and another five boxes of shotgun shells. "Yeah, that's enough."

THIRTY-ONE

I left Kelly's truck running while we loaded the guns and I put on the body armor. When I was ready, I followed Munroe out of the parking ramp and into the lot. The pickup truck had gone and I observed the driver had done a good job clearing the ramp. The way the snow fell though his effort wouldn't matter within the hour.

We drove back through the neighborhood and this time parked a block away from the house. I climbed out of Kelly's truck and made my way over to Munroe's passenger seat.

Munroe chewed a fingernail and scanned the street ahead. He turned on the radio, twisted through the stations and let it land on a talk show. After a minute he turned off the radio and sighed. "Most of the cruiser patrols will be tied up with traffic so you'll have about twenty minutes before anyone gets here. Once they get a shots fired call, they'll come at the house in full force."

"How many men inside?"

"A half-dozen maybe. They all look the same—heavy coats, heavy boots and they're all the same height—so hard to keep them separate."

I continued asking questions trying to get the layout of the house, what kind of guns they had, their skill level.

"Most of them don't practice shooting," Munroe said. "In the Army, they sent us to the range every six months, more if the budget allowed. These guys have a complicated initiation system involving tattoos in painful places, vouchering and background checks, but one thing I've never known them to do is spend any time at the range to prove they can shoot. They'll beat the living hell out of one another, they'll lift five-hundred-pound bench presses, but the guns are for show. Only two of them are any good and those only because they have seen actual military time in Russia."

"I assume anyone pointing a gun at me knows how to use it."

Munroe smiled. "That was the first thing they taught us in the academy." Then more seriously, "Shoot everyone. There's nobody innocent in that house."

Shoot everyone. I felt surprised by how calm and unimpressed I was by the statement.

An alley cut between the houses. Someone had plowed through it with a pickup truck, but the work was sloppy, not like the parking garage. Trash cans had been dented and knocked over. Black plastic bags had been cut open by the blade or trampled on by the tires as the truck moved back and forth clearing the alley.

"Ten minutes," Munroe said. "I'll give you ten minutes to get in place. You go up the alley, I go across the street. You ready?"

I nodded.

"Take care, John."

"You too, *Detective*."

"Randall."

"Randall."

He hit the timer on his watch and climbed out of the car. I watched him running low across the street, past garages and over trash. I looked down at my wrist. I didn't have a watch. I would have to move fast, find a place to hide, and wait.

I thought about Boris Egorov. I'd put two holes in his chest. I'd seen his back blow out and blood spray across the floor, his desk, a lamp shade. The image woke me up more than once in the last twelve years. Not because I felt guilt, but because it showed me all too well the fragility of the human body. A complex machine, capable of many things, but a spray of bullets could tear one up in a matter of seconds.

I pulled my gear from the back seat and mimicked Munroe's crouch-run up to the first garage in the alley. I leaned against the building and listened. The neighborhood was quiet. I couldn't even hear televisions. This time of year, all the windows were closed, but any sound would appear louder because of the emptiness of the streets and sound reflecting off the snow.

Munroe had given me a choice of guns so I picked a shotgun with eight shells in a holder on the stock. The previous owner, who had no skill with a hacksaw, had cut off the end in a jagged fashion. It added a bit of intimidation, but I didn't care about intimidating anyone. I had eight shells in the magazine tube and six in my pockets.

There was no moon, no stars overhead, just city lights reflecting on low hanging clouds.

A motion sensor light came on and I skirted around it. My breath hung in the yellowish light, my feet crunched in the snow and I felt like I was driving a semi-truck into a monastery.

I took my time moving closer to the house, but nobody came into the alley nor did I see footprints. No enthusiastic truck owner had cleared this far into the alley so I stepped through twelve inches of snow until I was behind the Russia House.

From the back, in the dark, the house was even more intimidating. I couldn't see a back porch and hadn't thought to ask Munroe if it had one. The windows appeared covered with tape and boards which allowed slivers of light through. A chain link fence blocked the way between the separated garage and the yard. I jumped the fence and leaned against the garage, trying to listen over my hammering heart.

Nobody came out. No lights appeared. No muzzle flash. I crouched low and looked around. Someone had struggled through the snow to move a trash bin near the garage. Their tracks disappeared in deep holes in the snow and the trash can stank of alcohol and cigarettes.

Cold crept into my feet and up my legs. I wondered how much time had passed. Was Munroe sitting warm inside the house watching the minutes tick off? How long had it been? Five minutes, six, less or more?

No movement came from the house. I considered moving closer. The smokers wouldn't come out, it was too cold. No deliveries would come on a night like this and no cars would come in from the alley. The cars out front could hold maybe a dozen men. Would that many be in the house?

An explosion rocked the sky over the house turning into a black cloud against the gray sky. The backyard lit up. Discarded tires and stacks of boxes filled the yard along with odd shapes under inches of snow. The house had a porch with balustrades wrapping around the entire first floor. Thick frost covered the windows preventing anyone from seeing out though someone had cleared piled snow from the window sills.

I put the shotgun up to my shoulder and ran to the

backdoor. Men yelling in Russian moved to the front of the house. Someone laughed. Another explosion, this time several of them swore in English. The explosion faded, and the light with it.

Through a head-high window on the door, I saw someone coming down the hallway towards me. I stepped to the side of the door and noticed the overhead light bulb appeared intact. I considered stepping to the side of the house, but waited. The light remained off as the door opened inward and the barrel of an AK-47 popped out. Suddenly the gun lit up and bullets sprayed across the yard, into the garage wall and into the alley.

More yelling from the front of the house. The gun barrel dropped, and the man yelled a response in Russian. I brought the butt of the shotgun up. He popped his head out and I slammed the butt of the shotgun into his face. He pulled the trigger of the rifle, bullets sprayed into the deck. I hit him again, and he dropped to the ground.

I stepped over him into a dark hallway. Wood stairs to the left. Plastic runners held in place with gold tacks ran along the stairs. To the right the kitchen was dark, but warm like the oven was on. Dishes filled the sink and a table in the center of the room had a few dishes laid out for a meal. I looked up the stairs, saw no light and moved forward down the hall.

I passed two rooms on either side. One looked like an office and the other like a makeshift bedroom with a couch and a military cot.

The front door was open. Several men stood in the doorway looking toward the burning house across the street. Pistols stuck from their waistbands. One of the men pointed into the street, apparently laughing at someone. Next to them, another man looked out a window. He held a cigarette in his left hand and a bottle of vodka in his right. A semi-automatic hung from a holster on his left side.

I couldn't see further into the room. If I shot them now, someone might come around the corner. No mirrors, no reflections, nothing to show anyone else was in the room.

One man at the door turned, saw me and paused, registering me as not being the person he thought I should be. He said something in Russian.

I pulled the trigger and his body exploded in red. The slug tore into his chest. The man standing next to him turned surprised. I pumped the next shell into the chamber and shot him. The slug hit him high in the shoulder and obliterated his collarbone. I couldn't hear the spent shells clicking to the floor, I couldn't hear anything. I didn't know if the men were screaming or crying or yelling for backup.

I crouched as I chambered the third shell. It was an awkward movement. I fell to the left as the third man drew his gun and fired. The fall saved me. The bullet tore up the wall behind me.

I squeezed the trigger jerking the shotgun in anticipation. The shell hit the man low in the gut. He twitched and bent forward, the gun falling from his hand as he clutched at the hole.

The first man had expected someone else—maybe the guy at the backdoor, maybe somebody from upstairs. Munroe said the house had two full floors and a partial attic converted into a sniper nest.

I picked up a gun, pointed it at the ceiling and pulled the trigger. I didn't expect the bullets to go through the floor, but I wanted the gunfire to confuse anyone upstairs. I ran to the stairs and fired twice into the second floor walls. I dropped the gun and readied the shotgun about chest high for anyone who might pop around the top of the stairs.

I had five shells left.

I hugged the right side of the stairs stepping not on the plastic but on what I thought would be the firmest part of the wood. I was right. The stairs were silent. I stopped midway up and listened. The furnace fired and forced air moved throughout the house.

Someone grunted something in Russian to my left. I climbed several more steps, fired into the door, swung right and fired again into the dark space.

Something heavy hit the floor behind the left door and it swung open. A man lay on the hardwood floor face down. Suddenly another man popped around the doorframe and sprayed machine gun fire, up- down and then left-right. I ducked to the left as wood and plaster sprayed the wall and stairs. The man was in front of me screaming, the gun low at his waist, his face contorted in rage, blood splattered across the front of his shirt. He fired twice and bullets spraying over my head. I squeezed the trigger; the slug tore through his body and sprayed the wall behind him with blood and guts. He stared at me with vacant wide eyes as he tumbled down the stairs.

The door of the room on the right stood open. A bright lamp sat on a desk and beyond it a couch was pressed against the wall.

In fluent English, a voice asked, "That you, Brogan?"

I pointed the shotgun at the lamp, squeezed the trigger, but missed. The slug smashed into the wall beyond.

Egorov laughed. "I didn't expect so many teeth. I never got the sense you had a backbone."

"You came to kill me. I'm being proactive."

"Did I? We both spent twelve years in prison. You for killing my brother, me for trying to be a Russian businessman. If I wanted you dead, don't you think you would be dead?"

"You wanted to do it yourself is what I figure."

"That would be true if I had cared about my brother. He was the bastard older brother. He got corrupted by your country: lazy and slow and mean. I was serious about being a businessman. I wanted to make money, nobody gets hurt making money."

"What about the attacks in prison? Those were both Russians."

"Not me, not mine. I didn't even care about you. I had...I had my own concerns."

I laughed. "You're telling me you never wanted to kill me?"

"I didn't care enough about you to worry about it before. But now, lines are drawn."

I tried to think through the situation, tried to understand it from Egorov's perspective, but he didn't give me the time. He stood up casting shadows across the room and came around the corner.

He was in his forties and gray haired. I'd said all of thirty words to the man. He'd loomed over my life for twelve years —a specter always around the corner ready to slice my throat.

He held a gun in his hand, a real cannon. He didn't know where I was and had pointed it in the wrong direction. He tried to correct, to swing it towards me, but I was ready.

I shot him in the chest with the last slug and stood there on the stairs watching him die.

THIRTY-TWO

I tossed the shotgun onto the ground and walked back the way I'd come through the alley and out onto the street. I was a convicted felon. My prints were everywhere. If the cops wanted to put this on me, they'd find me. But I didn't care. Let them come.

Kelly's truck was down the block but I stopped. At the other end of the street Charlie stood under the only working street light. She held the hand of a young boy, maybe eleven or twelve. She wore a long dress, white and curvy, under a thin coat open so I could see the dress. Red lipstick, perfectly placed, gave her a wet look. Her hair curled up, exposing one side of her neck. A thin silver necklace glittered under the light.

For just one minute I looked upon her not as what was, but what could have been. I remembered those twelve year old dreams—love, happiness, a family—with the woman I would wake up next to every morning. We'd share our days with our son; play ball, ride bikes, talking about his own hopes and dreams.

I saw it, experienced it and then felt its loss. The truth of those twelve years came back and a hole grew in my chest.

I walked to her. Under the light, she smiled and tentatively raised her hand as if to wave. I could hear police sirens in the distance.

"What are you doing here, Charlie?"

"I followed you. I knew what you would do. I knew what you had to do. For us. It was the only way."

"Who's the kid?"

"He's our son. I adopted him."

"You *adopted* him? No, Charlie, you kidnapped him. What's your name, son?"

The boy looked from me to Charlie. "Johnny Junior," he mumbled.

"No," I said, "Don't look at her, look at me. What's your real name?"

"Casey. Casey Hunt."

"Well, Casey Hunt, I need you to climb into that truck over there and keep your head low. We'll get you back to your real family soon."

Casey looked from me to Charlie and when she nodded, he went to the truck.

"You shouldn't talk to our son that way."

"He's not my son or your son. He's somebody else's son and they want him back."

"Are you mad at me, Johnny?"

"I think I've been mad at you since the day I met you, only I didn't see it in myself. Something was broken inside me and it took a hell of a long time to figure out what it was."

"I love you, Johnny."

"You don't know what that means. I don't think you see the world. I think you live inside your head and you move around doing things, all kinds of things, whatever kind of things just pop into your little brain. The world, people, they don't matter to you. You want something, you make it happen—mostly in your head. I didn't know it at first, but that's that one thing I hate, that lack of seeing the truth. I tried to show you, tried to make visible all those things you didn't see. But I didn't realize until now you don't live in this world with the rest of us. You only see what you want to believe."

She moved closer. "It's freezing out here. Can we get inside Lou's truck, please?"

"*Lou's truck?*" When she didn't respond, I said, "You stole the money from Tancredi and gave it to the Russian to get me out of prison."

"I don't know what you're talking about."

"Stop lying, Charlie. Just once see the world the same as everyone else. For one minute. Please just see the truth. You stole the money from Tancredi over months and paid the Russian to say he killed Boris Egorov. Were you at the shop the night I shot him? Did you pick up the gun when I dropped it? Somehow you got the gun into Chorkina's hands. Everything is so twisted up in your head that you thought it was the right thing to do."

She touched my chest, smiled up at me. Her lipstick was perfect. She smelled like a spring flower just bloomed. Her hand touched my coat. She sighed.

"You did a hell of a job," I said. "You put the Russians on me in prison. Why try to kill me?"

She shook her head. "I never tried to kill you, Johnny. I love you! I asked them to train you, keep you motivated. Prison can be hard. A man can wither away behind those walls. I needed you to stay hard. I needed my man to protect me when he got out, and it worked! Look how strong you are. You took on the Russian mob for me. I helped you,

Johnny."

"*Helped me?*"

"Don't you see? You beat them, all of them. You won. *We* won. I agree things didn't turn out perfect, but I did my best and everything worked out. The Russian didn't kill you after you killed his brother. He had no loyalty. He should have come here and fought you, but he didn't. He got arrested and stayed in prison. If we had killed him, I could have taken over the business. I could have used the money, the power to get you out. We'd *own* this city."

I took a long slow breath. The air was icy. The sirens were louder now. Munroe had said twenty minutes. We had less than five left.

"Tancredi was a misstep," she said. "A worthless bastard, he wanted real estate not power. He didn't see the money to be made. I tried to motivate him, but he only wanted to revitalize the city enough to control it. And I never loved him. I've only ever loved you, but this is a war and soldiers have a job to do. Right? You do understand how hard I've worked for us, right? I've spent years bringing us back together so we could start a family and run this city."

"How did you know that was Lou's truck?"

"Johnny, let's go home. We have everything we want. The whole city is ours! Let's look to the future not the past."

"Answer me."

She looked up into my eyes, her eyes glittering soft and warm. I'd spent years fascinated by the depths behind them.

"He stood in our way. He was trying to influence you. He wanted you to go a different path but we had a path, you and I. We were the future, not him, not that job as a mechanic. You were meant to rule this city as my king."

I thought about Sam. I thought about the photos in her living room, the ones with the scratches on the faces. "Did you go to Sam's house?"

She collapsed in my arms. "Johnny, why are you doing this? Why can't you stop? Stop thinking, stop worrying. We have everything. It's all complete, it's all ours. Just let it go!"

I grabbed her shoulders, shook her. "*What did you do, Charlie?*"

"I understand, Johnny, a man has needs. You weren't ready for me. You strayed, but I understand. You were in prison a long time, but I couldn't allow that to go on. You're my man. I couldn't allow another woman to get in our way. We have love. I couldn't let that woman come between us. I had to kill her, Johnny, I had to."

I let go of her. I stepped back. She slumped before me, her eyes sad, a tear wet her cheek. She wiped it away.

I clutched at the gun—her gun— in my pocket, pulled it loose from my coat and shot her. Her eyes widened. She glanced down at the hole, covered it with her hands and smiled. Her eyes narrowed, and she looked at me as if for the first time and there was sadness in them and understanding.

"A different path," I said.

She fell against me and I helped her to the ground. "Where is it?" I asked quietly in to her ear. "Where's the gun?"

I patted her down and found it in the left pocket, a small piece but enough to do the job of killing.

"You were last, Charlie, but you should have been first. I've never been right with you. Every step of the way I made the wrong play. Every step of the way I thought I was doing the right thing, but you manipulated every thought and action in my life. I was a stupid kid, and I got played hard because I was in love with you and I thought it would be all right. Maybe you do know what love is, because you understood how to manipulate it so well."

"Johnny, we can make this right. I know we can. We have to forgive. Forgiveness, that's what we need."

"There's no forgiving this."

She gasped. I laid her on the sidewalk, her feet propped up at a weird angle on the curb.

"Hospital," she whispered. "Please. It's freezing out here."

"You're going to die in the gutter where you belong."

"You're a bastard, Johnny."

"Only to you, Charlie."

THIRTY-THREE

I dropped the boy off at his house, a nice suburban home, and drove away in Kelly's truck trying not to see the parents hugging him in the review mirror. I had nothing left to do and now I had nowhere left to go. I was numb. Charlie had taken everything.

I did the only thing that made sense. I went back to the diner; the only decent place remaining, with a good memory of a good woman. I found a booth, and stared at the menu until it became too heavy and fell from my hands. Then I stared at the table, the rage, the hate—even the love—all gone.

"You came back," the waitress said.

I looked into her eyes, but I couldn't explain what I felt. How could I tell her what I had done?

Comprehension drifted into her eyes and then tears. I tried words, but none came. My mouth wouldn't move, my throat couldn't open.

"No," she said. "No."

I turned back to my scraped and blood covered hands.

"No," she said again, backed up and turned away. She disappeared behind the counter.

The room felt hot. I thought about the river—cold and black and peaceful. I started to rise from the booth when the waitress returned and said, "She can't be dead, I got this *yesterday*."

She shoved a postcard into my hand. One side had a picture of a mountain stream running cold and strong with the text *Cutter Springs* at the bottom. I flipped the card over. The diner's address with delivery to *Samantha*.

The waitress stood next to me nodding. Her name tag, clipped to her crisp white lapel, said *Mable*.

I pushed myself out of the booth, pulled Mable close and planted a big kiss on her lips. She squeaked. I let her loose, ran to the door and drove to Lou's as fast as I could.

I parked in front of the neighbor's house. A woman in her fifties answered my knock. She said hello over a dog barking from somewhere in the back.

"I'm here for Lou's dog."

She smiled. "He said you would come, though I expected you sooner."

"I got held up."

I waited while she brought the dog around with a leash and a small bag of rawhides.

"He's a good dog," she said. "We'll watch him any time."

I thanked her and guided the dog to the passenger side of the truck where he jumped in easily to the familiar territory. I had never owned a dog but then I had never owned many things.

It was time for change.

The dog wouldn't settle so I dug into the bag for a rawhide and found a stack of papers. While the dog gnawed on the rawhide I went through the papers. Lou had sold the land to an auction house the day before his death. Among the details I found a check from the sale made out in my name.

I stared at the check for a long time. Then, slowly, I put the papers and the check back into the bag, drove to a gas station where I found a map with a mountain on the cover.

The dog had finished half the rawhide by the time I drove over the bridge, the map and the postcard on the seat between us. I had the map open marking the route to *Cutter Springs*. The drive would take five hours if I drove the speed limit—I would do it in four.

No traffic passed me on the bridge. I stopped at the top, pulled the gun from behind the seat and separated the frame from the slide. A tow barge passed by filled with garbage. I waited impatiently and, once it passed, threw the pieces into the river.

I got back in the truck and turned down the heat. We had a long drive ahead of us.

About the Author

Tony Block grew up all over the American Midwest. When he was nineteen he joined the Marine Corps and got to see even more of the country and then the world. He currently lives in Boulder, Colorado with his girlfriend.

When he's not working on the next thriller, Tony reads, travels the country in his RV, and hikes the Rocky Mountains. He currently doesn't have a dog, but is considering getting one.

You can find out more at http://tonyblock.net.